Let Justice Roll

A Novel
Virginia Kreimeyer

But let justice roll like a river,
righteousness like a
never-failing stream.—Amos 5:24 (NIV)

iUniverse, Inc.
Bloomington

Let Justice Roll

iUniverse books may be ordered through booksellers or by contacting:

iUniverse
1663 Liberty Drive
Bloomington, IN 47403
www.iuniverse.com
1-800-Authors (1-800-288-4677)

Because of the dynamic nature of the Internet, any web addresses or links contained in this book may have changed since publication and may no longer be valid. The views expressed in this work are solely those of the author and do not necessarily reflect the views of the publisher, and the publisher hereby disclaims any responsibility for them.

Any people depicted in stock imagery provided by Thinkstock are models, and such images are being used for illustrative purposes only.
Certain stock imagery © Thinkstock.

ISBN: 978-1-4759-4221-7 (sc)
ISBN: 978-1-4759-4222-4 (ebk)

Library of Congress Control Number: 2012913920

Printed in the United States of America

iUniverse rev. date: 08/01/2012

Previous book by the author:

Sins of the Fathers—a novel set in the Balkans during the war among the Bosnian, Croatian and Serbian factions.

Dedication

This book is dedicated to my hard working mother—Loraine—who taught me justice in an unjust world. It is also dedicated to my loving husband—John—who so often became my muse, my inspiration, and mostly provided me the time and place to write. Finally, to my beautiful daughters, for it is my hope they will read it and share it with their children.

Acknowledgment

Although this book is based on a true story of what happened to a policeman and his new wife, the names and places have been changed to protect their identity. Additionally, a literary license has been taken to develop the characters and places, so that only the basis of the story remains true to life. I also want to thank my friends who read the book as I wrote it and helped me keep it real.

Chapter 1

In the heart of the South, there's a saying, passed from generation to generation, "to make Momma proud." For Savannah Whitehall, those words echoed from her earliest memories, for her and her sister, every time they walked out the door. But, today, the responsibility ingrained in her DNA "to make Momma proud" just might be more than she could muster. It might lead to accepting injustice in an unjust world.

Leaving Savannah still snuggled in the bed, Tom was up at the crack of dawn to get ready for his big event, the tri-state police training competition, which he lived for. In the shower Tom could see the entire course in his mind. He had trained for this and, now, he was ready.

By the time he finished showering; Savannah was making the bed and muttered just loud enough for him to hear her from the bathroom, "I wish I were going with you."

"But you'll be there when it counts," he replied.

"If only I had not taken that last call yesterday, I wouldn't have to go to work this morning," she whined remembering how this event had been on her calendar for months, blocked off and reserved with red ink.

However, a phone call, just as she was leaving her job as Director of Communications, University of Mississippi Medical Center, turned her plans upside down. A camera team, from one of the local television stations, missed the media day for the hospital's new wing and wanted to film it early the next morning.

"I have to do this because it is important for the hospital's reputation," she tried to rationalize. "We don't always have the opportunity to get coverage for positive stories."

"Hey, babe, don't worry about it. It's just the same when I have to go in on my day off," her husband tried to assuage her obvious guilt. "You're the hospital mouthpiece. You have to be there."

"I am the luckiest woman in the world," she cooed, hugging Tom before he headed out the door. "I have the most understanding husband and the handsomest husband ever."

"And one who loves you more than anyone," he replied. "I'll see you when you get there."

"Okay, hon, thanks for being you. Love you."

"Love you, too, bye."

After her shower, Savannah gathered a t-shirt, shorts, and tennis shoes for her gym bag, so she could change at the office. Once at the office, plans changed. The interview and tour of the new rehab center stretched from an hour tour to an in-depth explanation of how the facility was funded and the specialized equipment procured for rebuilding muscles and bodies. Three hours later she was in her fire-engine red Mustang barreling down the road with not even a second to spare.

B.J. Thomas crooned "Raindrops Keep Falling on My Head" from the car's radio announcing her arrival at the training site along with a billowing cloud of red dust. The gravel and hard, red clay road, through the piney woods of central Mississippi, did not invite strangers, but allowed access to the secure site, with the final obstacle near the point of entry.

"I made it," she thought as she smiled from ear to ear. "Now I can watch *my man* beat the socks off everyone else."

Despite her many accomplishments, Savannah suffered from self-deprecation. But, when it came to the hunk of an athlete she had married almost two years ago, her pride exceeded the ordinary. To her, he was the epitome of physical fitness, with drop-dead looks and a brain to match. Some days she marveled that she landed such a catch. Even though Savannah could hold her own in any beauty or physical competition, her upbringing differed from Tom. With a lithe five-foot-five frame, she had been a high-school track star, which allowed her to keep pace with his six-foot-two long-legged body when they ran with the Hash House Harriers.

Shortly after getting married, they joined the Harriers, as part of their fitness efforts, and were immediately dubbed the "Barbie and Ken" duo. At first, it was a jealous nickname Roger and Betty Thornton had given them, because, as a couple, they had been the "cute couple" until Savannah and Tom joined. However, the nickname stuck with the two blondes, because their attitude and enthusiasm for life overshadowed everything else. With the passing of time, the Thorntons warmed up to "Barbie and Ken" and enjoyed occasional dinners together since Roger was the Jackson Police Department spokesperson.

Standing in the heat of the noonday sun, with her golden hair cascading over the white collar of her salmon and aquamarine floral print, short-sleeved silk blouse, perspiration beaded across her forehead and in the crease of her elbow beneath the azure gabardine jacket draped over her left arm. Oblivious to the minute particles from the brownish-red clay adhering to the azure skirt and white pumps, which sank into the red dust, she positioned herself at the last barricade to watch Tom cross the finish line first—she knew he would.

"I really wish I had changed clothes," she thought as drips of sweat ran down her back. But she knew it would have delayed her even more—and she would have missed his awesome finish, as Tom came into sight.

Gazing up from beneath the semi-shade of a Southern pine, Savannah considered how Tom would scale the final obstacle—a 12-foot wooden wall on one side, followed by a two-foot wide gap, which required participants to thrust their bodies toward the crossbar fastened between two 10-foot high metal poles. Not an easy task—but Tom could easily do that and then swing from the crossbar to the pole. Doing the hand over hand bar to reach the upright pole and slide down to the ground, before dashing across the finish line 50 feet away, would be a piece of cake, she mused. She noted the muddy pit between the wall and the metal poles, but her mind's eye took Tom well over that trap—even though the head and shoulders murky mire could be a cushion for other members of the team, it would not capture Tom. She was watching and waiting for the triumph.

Tom, a member of Jackson's SWAT team, was nearly two minutes ahead of the other competitors as he approached the wall of boards. Turning up his speed, his sprint appeared to propel him up and over the wall with the momentum easily carrying him to the crossbar. His outstretched arms led his body to the top of the wooden structure while calculating the distance needed for his fingers to close around the galvanized steel bar with a firm grip. Then he turned his torso toward the upright pole on his right.

Savannah cheered, "Way to go Tom!" Her insides jumped up and down watching her man win the heat. To say she was proud of him was an understatement for how she felt about the man she married. She couldn't help chiding herself for getting here so late.

In that instant the policeman grabbed the crossbar with his left hand, and twisted around towards the sliding pole to complete his objective. His palms sweated like clam shells fresh from the ocean. A bucket load of sweat poured from his head, across his face and down his shoulders, soaking the gray JPD t-shirt. The salty substance stung his eyes. He blinked several times to clear his vision.

Clearing the waterhole, his fingers closed around the bar, but instead of suspending him above the red clay at the Rankin County Law Enforcement Training Center, the crossbar snapped. With his sticky, left hand still firmly attached to the metal bar, his body flew beyond the mud hole, and landed with a loud thud. There was no water, no mud, and no grass to cushion the fall, nothing to absorb the impact of 197 pounds of flesh traveling at a velocity of five feet per second. The mass of muscle, bones and fluid bounced against the Mississippi red clay. Crumbled, broken, and oozing blood, the mound of flesh curled into an unnatural "S" formation.

Savannah's jacket floated down into the dust, as her hands instinctively covered her mouth barely suppressing her scream. In a millisecond, her jubilance transformed to shocked grief.

Her body seemed to not respond to what her brain was saying, resulting in her movements feeling as if she were watching a movie in slow motion. Somehow, she stumbled across the patchy grass to reach the love of her life. Although it was only seconds, the entire event seemed like forever, as her eyes followed Tom's body to the wall, to the bar, and then to the ground. Her heart raced, but her body froze.

"Run and break his fall. Pick him up. Help him," her brain said, but her body refused to respond. The pounding in her chest only grew louder. She was only a few feet away from the obstacle, but it seemed like miles. Why wouldn't her feet move? They were moving, but just not fast enough. All she could feel was pain and helplessness. She had to do something, but nothing had ever prepared her for watching her love die before her face. He was a policeman and there were inherent risks, but dying in front of her was not what she expected.

Before her hand touched his bloodied one, an EMT gently took her shoulders and tenderly moved her aside.

Paramedics, from Rankin County, had won the toss today to provide the required support for training and multi-force competitions. The EMS team parked the truck in the grassy area underneath a chinaberry tree, near the finish line, giving them a prime spot to cheer for the home team. The medical teams vied for this duty, because it took them to a remote site where they enjoyed the scenery and normally fought off the boredom with a deck of cards. But they never forgot why they were there. Today it was for Tom.

Chapter 2

K eeping a stiff upper lip challenged her with every bone in her body riveting as her lips quivered. A sickly taste of bile swept up from her abdomen to her mouth when her soft grey eyes blinked back a flood of tears. The unusually warm rays zapped a single tear trickling down her bronzed cheeks. She was sure someone had taken a needle of Novocain and punctured her heart, letting the drug course her veins and numbing her entire body. It slowed her responses replaying the tape of the surreal events in her mind. With her body frozen, the only movement was the occasional trickle of water from eyes fixated on the lifeless body dusted with red clay, when it thudded against the dry ground raising a cloud of dust several inches high.

Unable to reach down and caress the bulging biceps or the bloodied face of the man to whom she had pledged her love in sickness and in health less than two years ago, Savannah's sheer willpower kept her from crumbling to the ground next to him. Without missing a beat, the paramedics checked his vital signs, placed support around his neck, and carefully rolled the long, lanky body up to slide the gurney underneath.

With a daily workout routine of running 5 miles, lifting weights and strength building exercises Tom never balked at any physical feat. But none of his Herculean strength enabled him to lift so much as a finger. His only movement generated from a wisp of air that stirred tufts of sandy hair sprouting through white gauze above the closed eyelids. Once his body was securely strapped on the gurney, the certified technicians hoisted it off the gravel and loaded it in the ambulance for transport to the hospital.

Absent-mindedly she kicked at the blood-and sweat-soaked pebbles, her only outward expression of grief, anger and panic. In inaudible tones she repeated her own mantra of, "God, how could this have happened?"

The sound of the siren brought her out of her daze in time to sprint to her car to chase the ambulance back to the hospital. With her tires kicking up loose pebbles, she sped down the gravel road to Highway 43. Forty-three took the entourage out to U.S. 80 and the Woodrow Wilson exit to UMMC. The ambulance's siren cleared the way for her allowing the dual overhead V-6 cam engine to roar through intersections.

"He can't die, Lord," she screamed as tears rolled down her cheeks. In the car she could yell at God, cry her eyes out, and let go of her emotions. "Why, why, why him? He's too young, too good, and I need him, God. Please, please don't let him die."

"If I were in the ambulance," she chided herself, "I wouldn't have to park the car and could be by Tom's side right now. But then I'd be without a car. Oh, well, too late now," she mumbled running for the door. Her mind focused on the mundane to deflect the reality of her pain. It was part of her defense mechanism to keep a stiff upper lip no matter what she faced. "I just can't seem to get there fast enough. I have to see him, hold his hand, and tell him everything will be okay. That's what he'd do for me."

The return trip to the hospital's emergency entrance cut the trip to the training site almost in half. Her straight skirt constricted her stride, but her heels hardly touched the ground, preventing her from tripping the automatic door and causing her to stop momentarily for the glass doors to retract.

As her daily domain, the UMMC, sat on top of a hill, that had once been a volcano but now overlooked one of the oldest and busiest intersections of Jackson—North State Street and Woodrow Wilson Avenue. The medical facility had grown and expanded to meet the needs of the times. From the urology department on the second floor facing south, Woodrow Wilson appeared to split the sloping grassy hill, taking the eye across the divide to an island of green and ending with the cold concrete of Bailey Junior High School.

From the west side of the seventh floor heart patients could see over the tops of the pecan trees to the hills and valleys of Millsaps College's prestigious Georgian academic structures in red brick. Across North State Street was War Memorial Stadium. The newest wing of the hospital dedicated to research labs and rehabilitation of orthopedic and neurosurgery patients spread out to the east. A nine-level, gated parking garage for employees brandished state-of-the-art facilities and connected to the new wing with a covered walkway. An overflow parking lot extended eastward beyond the garage and a pay by the hour parking lot seized a portion of the hospital's front lawn. The back of the hospital faced north where the emergency room entrance provided easy access from North State Street or Old Canton Road and ample parking for emergency vehicles. Situated at the corner of a major intersection, UMMC's easy access and renowned emergency room made it the first choice for the victims of a plethora of accidents—especially since Mississippi was one of the top 10 worst states for travel. Although the hospital provided extensive research facilities, it specialized in orthopedics and neurology. Both of these specialties combined with the emergency room technology and the constant flow of interns deemed it one of the best teaching facilities in the South.

Savannah spent many hours in the emergency room, sometimes escorting news media teams enamored with the pristine chambers that accepted bleeding and mangled victims of accidents, violent acts, and disasters. When she arrived, she anticipated the cacophony of nurses, doctors, and EMS techs—as they raced Tom to a receiving room. Almost as deafening as the noise had been, the silence from their departure echoed in her ears when she was left her standing alone in the hallway.

"Savannah, what are you doing here?" asked one of the nurses. "Do we have a big shot in ER today?"

Shaking her head, unable to utter the words, and on the verge of totally losing her self-control, she remained mum. This was not a trauma exercise or one of the many emergencies she had handled before. She was involved in this—heart, mind, and soul. It was her soul mate that was being treated—not someone with a big name, but a young man who had given her his name.

Lovingly known as "Big Mama," Miriam Weeks looked at Savannah's tear-streaked face. "No, that's not—," she stopped without completing the sentence, because Savannah's nodding head affirmed the unspeakable. The nurse knew what line of work Tom was in and the danger he faced, so it was not a surprise to an experienced ER nurse. Miriam walked over to her, put her arms around the trembling shoulders.

"Oh, you poor, baby," said Miriam Weeks, the charge nurse for ER for the last 15 years. To her everyone was "baby" or "honey." Standing almost six feet in her stockings and with an "in charge" attitude, the fifty-something African-American could intimidate anyone causing a ruckus in her hospital, not by size, but with one look. But for those who needed comfort, those wide shoulders and strong arms exuded competence and compassion.

"Baby, come here and tell me all about it," Miriam soothed.

The two women shuffled arm-in-arm into a private office away from the mainstream of the ER. Words were her business, but they escaped Savannah because her heart ached to be in the examining room, to comfort Tom. Miriam's strong hold on her prevented her from doing what part of her desperately wanted—to run out of the office and pursue the doctors regardless of what they would say. She knew them by name—the neurosurgeon, the orthopedic surgeon, and the radiologist—and they hovered over her husband's body in the small room across the hallway. They were where she wanted to be. She was not accustomed to being on the sideline—she was always in the middle of things.

Through sobs and gasps for air, Savannah kept herself together enough to find the words to recount the preceding events of the day. "It looks bad," she told Miriam. "I don't know what I'll do if he, you know."

"Well, honey, let's don't go there until we have to."

"I can't just sit here idly without knowing what's happening. This is just too much. What can I do?" she asked as she tried to think logically and organize her thoughts.

Miriam hugged her and let her cry into her shoulder for a few minutes. "There, there, honey, now you'll feel better," she patted her back.

"How about filling out some paperwork?" the younger woman asked wiping her eyes and nose with a tear-soaked tissue. Focusing on the task at hand was one of Savannah's strongest traits—part of making mama proud—but it also hindered her relationships. Her crisis training had embodied her with a calmness that she could turn on like a faucet to handle any task.

"I have all the forms you need right here," replied Miriam as she pulled out one of the file cabinet drawers. "You just sit here and fill in these blanks while I check on things across the hall."

"Thanks, Miriam," Savannah said with a pitiful smile. "You're a godsend."

"You might want to call his folks, if you haven't already," she suggested as she opened the door.

"Oh, yeah. You're right. I have been so focused on Tom that I didn't think about his parents."

Savannah dialed the Whitehall's home number, hoping to catch Mrs. Barbara Boyles Whitehall at home. A member of the country club set and Junior League socialite, Barbara filled her days with community activities while Billy Bob sold more cars than anyone else in the state—at least his dealerships did. Savannah let the phone ring four times before the maid picked up.

"This is Savannah; may I speak to Mrs. Whitehall?" she asked, using a quiet, soothing voice.

"I'm sorry, Miss, but she's gone shopping," replied Pearl, the Whitehall's maid.

"Please ask Mrs. Whitehall to call my cell phone as soon as she returns. I am at the hospital and need to speak with her as soon as possible. I know she never answers her cell phone or I'd call it."

"Yes, Miss Savannah. I will, but it may be a while."

"That's okay, Pearl. But, it's really important."

"Yes, Miss. I'll tell her as soon as she returns."

"Thanks. Bye."

She had maintained a professional tone and kept her voice at an even keel. She didn't want to sound alarmed. She also knew that her calls to Barbara were infrequent enough that Barbara would most likely respond immediately. Tom usually called his mother if there was news to share as did Savannah hers. She dialed her mother's office number, but had to leave a message with the receptionist. Neither of their family lifelines was immediately available for the crisis. And neither of them liked using their cell phones. They were for their use, not for others to call them. For a communicator like Savannah, it was a difficult concept to comprehend, but like many other quirks of both her mother and mother-in-law, she simply accepted them for who they were.

When she looked up from the phone call, Miriam was standing in the doorway with a scowl on her face.

"Bad news?" queried Savannah.

"Well, it isn't good," she replied in her nurse voice with her arms akimbo. "They're taking your husband to

13

surgery now. He's still unconscious, and the X-rays indicate fractures to the C-spine as well as a broken femur and tibia. Dr. Pendleton is assisting with the surgery. I'm sure he'll be able to tell you much more."

Savannah bowed her head and prayed silently not just for her husband, but also for the surgeon and his team. She wanted Tom back, whole and healed, but her faith allowed her to add, "But Thy will be done, Lord. Because I know that in all things everything works together for the good of them who love you, Lord. Tom and I love you and trust you and praise you in all things, even times like this."

When she finished her prayer with "amen," Miriam added her "amen" as well. The tears had dried up, but her eyes still had telltale redness. Even in the midst of the crisis, after her prayer, a feeling of comfort and peace enveloped Savannah. In her resolve to deal with the unthinkable, her stress coping mechanism turned her thoughts to a philosophical discussion of life.

"Miriam, do you play cards—you know solitaire or gin rummy?" she began.

"I'm not much of one to play solitaire, but I've played some gin rummy or hearts before. I grew up playing cards with my family on Saturday evenings."

"Well, when I'm stressed out, I often play a game or two on my computer, just to let my mind wander. It keeps my hands busy, but lets me presuppose ideas and make analogies about life. Sometimes it helps me to problem solve difficulties."

"What do you mean, honey?"

"To me life is a lot like a game of cards," she said. "You get dealt a hand to play with and then you make choices based on what might make it better. It's just that sometimes, you make the wrong choices and when you do, you lose. Or, at least, lose out on what would be best. God gives us choices to make in life and even allows us to make the wrong ones. When we do, there are consequences, but He often gives us second chances."

"So maybe you don't really lose the whole game, just that hand."

"Well, that's true, because if you believe in Jesus as the way to eternal life, you know the end game results. But each choice can change the course you take," she countered letting the discussion consume her and diverting her despondency.

"Right! But isn't it the end game that counts?"

"If so, then the means justifies the end. So, actually it's not only how it turns out, but also how you play the game."

"You mean like following the rules?"

"Well, yes. But in the game of life, justice is not always served. We don't always get what we deserve and I'm grateful for that. If true justice was meted out, we might not be able to take it. So, thankfully, what we deserve is discipline, not the blessings we receive. Furthermore, the end game assures us of blessings and not suffering. But while we are playing the game of life, there will be suffering. You know like in football the players take hits every time they line up, but the choice of the play can make a difference as to how the ball moves down the field. One choice can mean that the offense gains yardage, while another choice means the defense pushes the ball carrier back yardage. It still comes down to the choices we make."

"So, are you thinking that this is a bum hand God has given you today?"

"Well, on the surface it certainly appears to be, but God can see past today and tomorrow. So, I need to play this 'bum' hand according to His rules."

"And how is playing the hand according to His rules going to get you through the day?"

"I believe God allows you to renege. You know like if you forget to follow suit and play the wrong card. Well, even though we deserve judgment for our mistakes, God has a plan that goes beyond justice and righteousness. God's justice is not the same as what we consider justice. He is righteous and cannot look on our sin, so He does not hand down the justice we deserve. He allows justice to roll like a river throughout our lives. By trusting God, it will all work out according to His best"

"I'm a woman of faith, honey, but what you're saying takes a lot more faith than I have right now."

"I have to. Otherwise I couldn't sit here and talk to you. I'd just be going crazy. You see, God gave Tom to me, but I have to show God that He is still number one in my life, just as Tom puts God first in His life. At least now he does. It hasn't always been that way."

"You mean Tom became a Christian only recently?"

"Not exactly. Tom and I have known each other since we were toddlers. We both grew up in Sunday school at First Baptist, but he was there because it was the socially correct thing to do. At first he came because his mother and father brought him so his dad could make deals and his mother connect with her social network. He made a profession of faith when he was eight because that was what was expected of him. And as a child he believed in God, but his belief was a carnal belief, not heart led belief."

"What's the difference?" Miriam asked curiously as she shuffled the files in her arm.

"Well, you can believe that there is a God and that He created the universe and everything in it, but not know Him in your heart. That's called 'head' knowledge of Jesus. But when you make Him, 'Lord of your life,' it means that you turn over your life to Him. You trust Him to know what is best for you because He loved us so much that He sent his only son, Jesus, to pay the price for us. When you see how much God wants to be with us—He created us for fellowship with Him, and then you trust Him to know what is best. Like most parents, God wants only the best for us. But we don't always choose what is best."

"You're back to the game of cards, aren't you?"

"Yes, because God gives us a free will to decide what we will take and what we will choose."

"So, what are your choices today?"

"Well, I can be angry about this or I can look for how God can be glorified through this difficult time. In the book of Job, Job was tested and proved his righteousness, even though his wife told him to 'curse God and die.' His extreme tests, losing his herds, his children, and his place of respect in the community, caused him to question God. But, he never questioned God's sovereignty. So by keeping my faith in God and realizing His sovereignty over life and death, I have to place not only my life, but also Tom's life in His hands."

"Whew, that's some faith you have, child," exclaimed Miriam. "I'll have to do some thinking about that one. Meanwhile, why don't you fill out these forms, so the paperwork police won't be breathing down my neck?"

A nurse opened the door to Miriam's office. "Sorry to interrupt," she said, "but we need you out here Miriam."

"Honey, we'll have to finish this discussion some other time. But I do want to hear your explanation. That's more than I've heard in my church going days."

"Sure, Miriam. Thanks for your help. See you later."

Returning her attention to the admitting and insurance forms, Savannah began filling in the blanks. The dialog had been therapeutic for her and kept her mind busy. By concentrating on the forms now, she didn't have to reflect on the day's events, but the information required for the arduous task. For more than half an hour she read instructions and inked data in the blanks. Facing the next few hours would be difficult. It was a waiting game—waiting for the surgery to be over and waiting for the prognosis.

Chapter 3

S avannah sat alone with the slate blue walls exacerbating the sterile loneliness of a hospital waiting room. There were well-worn magazines on the lamp table and a TV with the sound off but closed captions crawling across the bottom, but none of it was inviting or soothing to her. She escaped the contrived serenity by allowing her mind to wander to happier times with Tom, and there were plenty.

Vividly she recalled the day she and Tommy had their first real conversation. As seniors at Murrah High School they were selected as the Daughters of the American Revolution Good Citizenship awardees. The DAR honored them at the annual reception one afternoon at an antebellum house on North State Street. The night before the reception, Tommy called her and asked if she'd like to go with him to the event the next day.

"Sure, I'd really appreciate a ride," she said. "I was going to have to take my mom to work, so I could have the car. But, if you take me, that will be great."

"So, do you want to meet me out in front of the school at one o'clock?" he asked. "I'll be in a blue Mustang with the top down."

"Okay, but would you mind putting the top up, so the wind won't blow my hair?"

"Not a problem," he said as he chuckled. "I don't have enough hair to worry about."

"If I pulled mine back into a pony tail, I wouldn't have to worry either. But I don't think that'd be appropriate for the DAR and the ladies might not approve."

"I'm sure you are right. So, I'll see you tomorrow."

"Okay. And thanks for the ride."

"Glad to. Bye."

Savannah remembered how pleased she was with his politeness.

The next day promptly at one o'clock he pulled up in front of the school to pick her up. In true Southern gentlemanly fashion, he walked around the car to open the door for her. Once again she was impressed by his manners that warm October day.

"Don't you play the flute?"

"Yes, how did you know?"

"Oh, I have my ways," he replied as he winked and smiled at her. "I've seen you at some of the football games."

"Really? I've seen you at all the football games," she teased.

"Yeah, I guess I'm kinda hard to miss when I'm calling the plays."

"I hear Ole Miss has offered you a scholarship. Are you going to take it?"

"That's where my dad went to school. But I really want to go to Southern."

"Southern? That's where I plan to go, hopefully on a band scholarship. But why would you rather go to Southern instead of Ole Miss?

"For starters, it has a great criminology department and that's what I want to major in—not football."

Yes, Tommy Whitehall had impressed Savannah Canfield in ways she had never anticipated—with his honesty and academic inclination. Her pedigree was not the same as his, but her family had standards, too.

A second generation Jacksonian, her mother moved to Jackson after high school to attend Draughn's Business College. As a young woman Mary Ann Chambers joined the First Baptist Church, where she met and fell in love with Bryan Canfield. They were married at the church and later brought their two daughters, Elizabeth and Savannah, to their church.

Mary Ann worked from the time she was 16 until Elizabeth was born. After five years as a homemaker, she returned to work when Savannah's father died in a car wreck. Her secretarial training at Draughn's and years of experience prepared Mary Ann for the hand life dealt her. There was no choice and she was grateful for the preparation that landed her a job at a law firm for twenty-five years. It was the uncertainty of the future that taught Mary Ann a difficult lesson in life and she wanted to make sure her girls were prepared for life with their own careers and spiritual upbringing at her church.

First Baptist was the same church where Tom and Savannah met in the cradle department. However, they didn't *discover* each other until they were toddlers when they wanted to play with the same set of blocks at the same time. It was one of their first lessons in sharing at a place outside of home, as a much repeated antic told by Mrs. Emma Appleton. A beloved fixture in the church nursery for more than 40 years, Mrs. Appleton knew all the good, the funny, and the not so well-received anecdotes of children who grew up at her church. When a prominent family, like the Whitehalls, was involved, she took special delight in remembering the stories. Owning the largest Ford dealership chain in the state of Mississippi, Mr. and Mrs. Billy Bob Whitehall and their two sons, William Jr. and Thomas were considered very prominent.

In junior high school, the youngest Whitehall boy became Tommy, a football hero at Bailey Junior High with a student body of more than 400. Savannah could not help but know his name. However, her interest in music, both singing with the chorale and playing the flute in the marching band, prevented their paths from crossing often.

Their commonalities included running track, but since girls and boys never practiced or competed together, they rarely saw each other. At football games he was on the field and she was with the band in the stands. At church, Sunday school classes were segregated into girls and boys diminishing her opportunities to get to know him except for fellowships with the youth group.

Because they were both active in extracurricular activities at school and church, the DAR had selected them for the award. And even though their spheres of influence overlapped, specific interests had separated them until that sunny October afternoon.

Two days later Tommy called again.

"Hi Savannah, how's it goin'?" he asked, striving to be casual.

"Great. How about you?"

"Great. That DAR reception was really nice," he said stalling for words.

"Yes, I thought those ladies were a hoot. They take so much pride in their heritage. It's nice to see people respecting their ancestors like that. And the stories they told about their relatives! Can you believe them?"

"They were something. Say, homecoming is in two weeks and I was wondering if you have made plans for it."

"Well, other than playing in the band, no I haven't thought about it."

"Umm, well, I'll be playing in the game."

"I hope so, if we plan to beat Chastain."

"Yeah, well, I was thinking about after the game. Would you like to go to the dance with me?"

"Sure. That'll be great," she managed to stammer out without being too flabbergasted.

"So, can we meet after the game at the entrance to the gym? I'd pick you up earlier, but we have to be on the field."

"That's okay. I have to be in the band room early for practice. So that'll work for me."

"Okay, see you then."

"You bet, Tommy. Bye."

A smile crept across her face remembering how elated she was. For the next two weeks her feet never touched the ground. She couldn't believe she was going to homecoming with Murrah's star quarterback, who was not only the most handsome boy in school, but also was a genuinely nice person. In her book, he was an incredible person, and she was on cloud nine. From that moment on she knew she loved Tommy.

Murrah beat Chastain in the homecoming game with Tommy passing for four touchdowns and scoring one for the final score of 35 to 10. After the game Tommy met Savannah bearing the most beautiful powder blue orchid she had ever seen. It matched the blue taffeta with an empire waist that rose on one side in a collection of pleats and connected to the high bodice in the back, bared one shoulder, and amplified the blue hues of her grey eyes. The powder blue cummerbund of Tommy's black tux matched her dress impeccably.

They danced to a small local band that played mostly old rock 'n roll songs, with only a few oldies like "Cherished" and "You've Lost That Lovin' Feeling," to slow the music down. Her early childhood dance lessons paid off as Tommy glided her around the dance floor. Many eyes were on the couple in blue. It was a night she never forgot—a night of new beginnings—not just for their senior year, but for life.

Both attended Southern where Tom played second-string quarterback as a freshman for the Golden Eagles and started the next three years. They found little time to date with heavy academics and extra circular activities like his football and her demands for the band. As a music and communications double major, Savannah's work on the newspaper and in the band required her to attend summer school. Additionally, her internship with the *Hattiesburg Sun* and the six weeks she spent as a PR intern for Hill + Knowlton in London kept her tied up for long periods. For the aspiring PR professional, both were both experiences of a lifetime and contributed to her selection for the UMMC position.

Despite Tom's academic achievement, graduating summa cum laude in criminology, it was his prowess on the football field that made Billy Bob Whitehall proud. His senior year at Southern was a crowning success by leading the Eagles to the

SEC conference title and the bid for the Sugar Bowl in New Orleans on New Year's Day. The entire family made the trip to New Orleans to watch Southern play Nebraska. Although Tom completed more than 130 yards passing and rushed for 65, the result was only two touchdowns, which were not enough to beat Big Red. The defense couldn't stop the Red machine and the final score was Southern 14 and Nebraska 42. For his extraordinary effort, Tom earned the MVP award and a second round draft pick by the New Orleans Saints. At the chagrin of his father, Tom turned down the opportunity to play pro ball to join the Jackson Police Department. None of this bode well with the Whitehalls, since Billy Bob had high expectations of exploiting his son's football heroism as advertising for his dealerships. In the six years since Tom had announced his plans to the family, relationships had been strained.

"Mrs. Whitehall?" the surgeon asked from the doorway bringing Savannah back from football to the hospital.

"Yes," replied Savannah getting up from the burgundy and grey plaid cushioned chairs in the waiting area outside the surgery suites. The hours had seemed like days on end, waiting and waiting. In the seconds that followed she asked herself why she had not heard from her mother or mother-in-law. Looking at her watch, she realized it had been more than three hours since she had left her messages.

She really wished her mom were here; she was always a comfort to Savannah. Now the petite young woman faced a grim looking doctor by herself. She squared her shoulders, expecting the worst, but hoping for the best.

"Mrs. Whitehall," Dr. Pendleton began. "Let me give you the bad news first. We know his spine has been damaged, the third and fourth vertebrae were shattered in the fall and the C-spine suffered fractures. We were able to make repairs, but won't know until he regains consciousness the extent of his paralysis. With our technology, we were able to repair the apparent nerve damage and his broken limbs. I can't give you a clear prognosis yet, but with his excellent physique and rehabilitation, we can certainly expect a recovery. Right now it is just a wait and see state."

"Can I see him?

"Yes, he is in recovery. Let me take you to him."

In silence the two walked down the hall, turned left and pushed open the swinging doors to the room alive with mechanical sounds. Tom lay on the metal gurney, attached to IV tubes, and using a respirator to breathe. Bound in gauze, his head was supported by a halo, and his body kept rigid by traction poles attached to the gurney. With his eyes closed, the pallor appearance of his normally bronzed face distorted his features. Resolutely, Savannah walked to Tom's side, leaned over the rail, and brushed his cheek with her lips and began gently stroking the exposed surface of his face.

"Tom, I'm here, my love. I love you and I will always be here for you," she whispered to an ear covered with gauze.

"Mrs. Whitehall, you are welcome to stay here as long as you like. The nurses will let me know if there is any change in him. When there is, I will be back," assured the doctor.

He motioned for the ICU nurse to follow him out the door where they whispered before the doctor left the area.

Savannah's cell phone began vibrating in the purse dangling from her arm. She walked outside the room to take the call—a habit she had of being courteous to those around her.

"This is Savannah," she replied automatically.

"Well, this is Barbara," replied tersely. "You called?"

"Uh, yes, I did. Barbara, I'm at the hospital."

"So?"

"I'm here with Tom."

"Don't you mean Tom is with you?"

Barbara could be so caustic at times. It only made it more difficult for Savannah to tell her mother-in-law what had happened to her baby boy. But she managed to explain that Tom had been hurt and had not yet gained consciousness.

"I suppose you want me to come and sit until he does, so you can go to your job?"

"Well, actually, no. I just wanted you to know how serious this is. I have no plans to leave his bedside."

"Oh. Well, I'll see you shortly."

It wasn't exactly the response she expected. She thought the woman would have been hysterical and insisted that she be in charge. But then, Savannah didn't explain everything for fear of really upsetting her.

A few minutes later her phone vibrated again. This time it was Savannah's mother and her response was to comfort Savannah.

"Savannah, I'll be there to sit with you."

"That would be so wonderful. I know I am here every day, but it seems so cold and impersonal now. I'm not sure I can deal with this and Tom's mother, too."

"I know honey. She can be abrasive, but you know she loves Tom and you."

"I know she loves Tom, but I'm not so sure about me. I don't think she has ever accepted me into her family. I really can't say why. Anyway, I need you here. How long will it take for you to get here?

"I've been taking dictation, so all I have to do is straighten up my desk and drive over. That should only take 15 to 20 minutes."

"Good. You should be here before Barbara."

"Yes, I will. See you in a few."

"Okay. I love you, Mom."

"Love you, too, honey. Bye."

Savannah took a deep breath and let it out. Her shoulders relaxed a bit. Her heart still ached for Tom, to see him smile and wink at her. At least she would now have an ally with her mom here. She began to contemplate the worst-case scenario for Tom. What if he doesn't wake up? She couldn't bear to think the unthinkable. Refocus she told herself.

Life was special to the couple and they cherished their limited time together. They often left *love notes* for each other by the coffee pot in the kitchen. After waiting until college and his police training were completed to be together, they savored their time. This morning Tom left her a note:

> *See you when I win.*
> *It's Savannah's smile,*
> *That gets me to the end.*
> *Love you—in a while?*

That was one of the reason Savannah had made an extra effort to be at the competition. Most wives weren't there, but Savannah was. With Tom's bandaged hand in hers, her mind's eye returned her to the training camp.

A sea of blue entered the hospital. Heels clicked down the hallway as the crisp squad rounded the corner to Tom's room.

"Hello, Savannah," came a solemn greeting from a tall, thin blond in his starched midnight blue shirt.

"Oh Chris," Savannah countered but glad to see a familiar face. "It's so awful."

"I know, but we are here to support you," replied Chris O'Donnell one of JPD's internal affairs sergeants. All three attended high school together, but didn't run in the same circles of friends. Although they were brothers in blue, since Chris had moved from the SWAT team to IA, the two former football players hardly saw each other.

Carrying a beautiful mother-in-law's tongue, officially called sansevieria trifasciata, literally translated as snake plant, Chris leaned over to place the plant embedded in a royal blue ceramic ewer on the hospital table.

"What do you know about his prognosis?"

"It isn't good, but they won't know the extent of some of the injuries until he wakes up."

"Have they given you any idea of when they expect him to?" Chris asked with a furrowed brow denoting deep concern.

"Not really. Right now the doctors are working on patching up his broken bones and lacerations."

"Well, let us know what we can do to help. We are here for you, Savannah. Anything you need, just let me know," he said handing her his business card. "I've written my personal cell on the back so you can call me anytime."

With that Chris and the four blue uniforms marched out of the room leaving Savannah to struggle silently with her emotions. Chris was the only one she recognized and somewhere in her psyche she noted that it was Chris and these strangers who had visited the hospital. No one but Chris had spoken a word to her. Curiously she wondered why someone from the SWAT unit had not been there. But she dismissed it because the team must still be tied up with the competition.

"Savannah, your mother's here," announced the nurse.

Pushing the heavy swinging door open, Savannah practically fell into her mother's open arms. It was a relief to let her guard down, even for a brief time, and her mother was such a comfort.

"Mom, it was so awful. I saw the whole thing! I can't believe this happened to Tom," she sobbed into her mother's shoulder.

"Well, tell me what you need me to know and the rest we can talk about later," her mother said patting her hair.

Recounting the details of the afternoon gave Savannah a new perspective as they sat in the hospital chairs next to each other.

"I can't imagine why that metal bar would break away from the post like that," she heard herself saying.

Mary Ann just listened as her daughter talked, sobbed, and dabbed her eyes with her tissue. All the while she patted Savannah's hand and thought about the harrowing experience her youngest daughter had encountered. She knew the most important thing she could do was listen.

She had been the strong support for her girls, trying to fill the role of both mother and father. As a working mother it was not easy, because she often had tough choices to make to provide a moderate lifestyle. She was proud of the woman Savannah had become, proud of her successful career, and proud of her life as Tom's devoted wife. They had had many conversations about this young man her daughter loved more than self. Savannah didn't say the words, but Mary Ann knew that if she could have taken the fall instead of

Tom, Savannah would have. It was an unconditional love, selfless and persevering that resonated in this young woman for *her man*. She had once experienced that kind of love and understood it. She prayed that Savannah wouldn't have to face the loneliness she had in the last 20 years.

Did history repeat itself? She wondered what would happen to Tom.

Barbara dutifully came to see Tom, but left after getting a report on his condition. Mary Ann buffered the encounter for her daughter much as a diplomat between sparring nations. After Mary Ann went home, Savannah was again alone with Tom in a semi-lit room. A sharp knock on the door startled her.

"Hi, Savannah. I heard the news and just stopped by to check on Tom," explained another uniformed policeman. Pat O'Brien, Tom's partner when they were on the beat in West Jackson, looked at the tubes and machines and shook his head. "Man, I can't believe this happened to Tom," he commented and handed Savannah a small potted geranium.

"I know. Neither can I," she said standing on the opposite side of Tom's bed. Pat only stayed a few minutes, but extended his help to Savannah. She thanked him for coming, although she was surprised that he knew about the accident already. However, news does travel fast throughout the JPD. But she mulled, he said he was on his way to work the evening shift and had not yet been to the station.

Chapter 4

It had been almost three weeks since Tom's accident and he still had not regained consciousness. Savannah went to see the neurosurgeon.

"We've repeated the X-rays and the cranial scan," Dr. Pendleton explained. "Both show some brain activity, but not much. Still, this is hopeful. But in cases like this we can never accurately predict when he will be out of the coma. It may be days or weeks or months."

"Thanks, Dr. Pendleton, for being so candid. He's now in God's hands. And we'll have to wait and see what His will is."

"We don't want to leave him here in ICU, so we'll transfer him to the rehab center in the east wing. But it's your call as to how soon we do it."

"Let me think about this. I know I'll have to discuss it with his folks."

Savannah turned and walked towards the elevators that took her to the main lobby. From there she took a covered walkway to the south section of the hospital where she rode an elevator to the administrative offices on the eighth floor. As the Director of Public Relations for UMMC, her purview included a small suite of offices off the main corridor. Windows facing Woodrow Wilson Avenue lined the south wall of her office, which included a small conference table. When she first moved into the office, she had been mesmerized by the constant traffic flow. But the steady rumble no longer attracted her attention. Only violent storms, like the notorious tornados that were spawned by hurricanes in the Gulf, directed her attention to the huge double-paned windows. But when she was particularly troubled or in a deep conversation on the telephone, she often paced in front of the windows. She dialed Barbara's number to give her the latest on Tom and turned to face the windows where the April showers gently tapped the panes.

"Barbara, this is Savannah. I just wanted to let you know about my latest conversation with Dr. Pendleton. He says there is no improvement in Tom's condition. The X-rays and cranial scan show minimal brain activity, but he really has no prediction as to when Tom will come out of the coma. He suggested that we move him from ICU to the rehab center."

"Really? And what did you say?"

"I told him I wanted to discuss it with you and Billy Bob first."

"Well, that's the first sensible thing you've done during this entire situation."

Savannah had a sharp comeback, but held her tongue. It would only make matters worse and she really didn't want to alienate Barbara. She took a deep breath and waited.

"I can't believe you went back to work with poor Tom still in a coma. If he were my husband, I'd have been there with him every day."

"But Barbara, I'm right here in the hospital and only minutes from him, if there is any change at all. The nurses can call or page me and I can be at his side almost immediately. I'm at the hospital all day and spend every moment I can with him. That's why I thought moving him to rehab would be good. They can begin to work his arms and legs to prevent atrophy."

"Well, there is a better place in Atlanta, one that specializes in multiple trauma care. And that's where Billy Bob and I want him. We want the best we can find."

"I don't think our insurance will pay for something like that and we have a great rehab center here."

"Did I ask you to pay for it?"

"Well, no, but . . ."

"I said Billy Bob and I would take care of it. Besides, it's all arranged. Billy Bob has a business associate who found out that the Atlanta Medical Center has the best doctors in the country. We'll put him on the company jet and fly him down on Monday."

"Monday? But, Barbara, how can you do this without talking to me?"

"Well, I can. So, if you want to see him everyday, you'll just have to quit that precious job of yours. Your place is at his side, not at work. If you were the right kind of wife, that's where you'd be."

"What do you mean, 'the right kind of wife'? I love Tom and would do anything for him."

"Then prove it. Quit that job or yours and go with him to Atlanta."

"Barbara, you know I can't do that. We have bills to pay and someone needs to earn money to pay them."

"If you hadn't kept him from playing pro ball, you wouldn't have bills to worry about."

"How can you say that? It was his decision not to play with the Saints. I just supported what he wanted."

"Well, now his father and I are stepping in to make sure he is taken care of properly."

"I can't believe you're doing this!"

"Well, believe it, honey," she said, her words dripping with sarcasm. "I'm going to see to it that somebody takes care of my baby boy. We'll be at the hospital bright and early Monday morning. Goodbye."

With that Barbara slammed the phone down before Savannah had time to say, "Goodbye." She was stunned. Didn't she have rights as the wife? She called her mom at Brown, Pierce & Southerland or BPS Law Firm, which specialized in civil and criminal law cases, to find out what recourse she might have.

"Mom, can I get an injunction to stop them?" she asked. "Is there anything I can do?"

"Well, honey, I'll check with my boss and see what we can do. But this is Friday afternoon and to do something by Monday morning; it's next to impossible."

"But, Mom, you've got to try. I just can't let Barbara ship Tom off to Atlanta, even if they do have the best rehab center in the nation."

"I understand, but I'm not sure what Mr. Brown can do. I'll call you as soon as I know something. Meanwhile you can pray about this."

"I will, Mom. And thanks."

Immediately Savannah visualized a terse moment shortly before Tom and Savannah were married. Barbara, Tom and Savannah were in his mom's dining room where they were finalizing wedding plans. A discussion over the limited invitation list had erupted and Barbara announced, in front of Savannah, that Tom was, "marrying beneath our social status."

"Maybe Savannah's family doesn't have money, but they still have class," Tom retorted. "And I know Savannah is a classy lady. More importantly, I love her and she loves me. That's what really matters."

It was the first time Savannah had seen Tom stand up to his mother, because he was normally very respectful to her. She resolved to make sure she didn't give Barbara reasons to degrade her in the future. However, with the wedding being a small, intimate affair because Savannah paid for it herself, Barbara acted miffed that she couldn't invite all her society friends. Savannah secretly thought that it was all show and that Barbara was really relieved they didn't have to flaunt Tom's bride in the face of their friends. As a policeman, Tom's salary was nowhere near what Willie made as their father's protégé on the Coast. So, instead of an expensive honeymoon, Tom suggested his parents contribute to a down payment on a house. Billy Bob was all for that idea, and without his wife's approval, laid out a handsome mortgage investment on a modest townhouse on the Ross Barnett Reservoir.

For Tom and Savannah having a child was a distant desire because they had their dream jobs and wanted to establish themselves in their respective professions. This had created another rift between Savannah and her mother-in-law. Tom's brother was married to a former debutante whose father was a U.S. representative for the Gulf Coast district. And Willie was the general manager for two of the Whitefield Ford dealerships in Gulfport and Biloxi. Willie and Becky lived the society life on the Coast and their little princess with her twin brothers captivated Barbara's heart.

Savannah knew she had only complicated Tom's life, but that was their lot in life. Love conquered most things and for her and Tom, the risk of being estranged from his parents was worth the life Tom chose with Savannah. Regardless of the demands of college and the snubbing she had often felt from Barbara, Savannah knew Tom was happy. She could see it in his eyes when he looked at her. She could feel it in his fingertips when he stroked her face. And she knew her deep love for him was unfaltering, regardless of the obstacles of life. Sometimes they were like ships passing in the night, especially when he had worked the 11 to 7 shift. He left for work when she went to bed and she was either leaving or had already left for work when he came home.

Now Savannah had to stand up to Barbara by herself. She did not enjoy being confrontational, but recognized opportune circumstances. She quietly prayed for strength and discernment for the right action.

"Lord, I just come to you now, recognizing you as my sovereign Lord and praise you as my Father in heaven who watches over me. Now, I ask that you grant me wisdom and discernment to know what to do and say. I claim your promise that if we lack wisdom, all we have to do is ask. And I ask for the strength to do your will so you will receive the praise and glory through my life. I know that I can do all things through Christ who strengthens me. In your Son's name I pray. Amen."

When she raised her head and opened her eyes, her administrative assistant was standing at the door.

"I'm sorry to interrupt you, but Dr. Pendleton is on the phone," said Wanda Crutchfield, a small, wiry woman with efficiency expert pervading her presence. Wanda pulled her hair back into a tight bun at the nape of her neck and peeked over granny half-frames at everything except her reading material. With a pen in the hand she had wrapped around a spiral notebook and the other on the doorknob, her black A-line dress with white collar and cuffs spelled business with a capital "B."

Savannah didn't know how long Wanda had been standing there, or if she had heard the conversation with Barbara. No matter. Wanda was not a gossip. And she didn't spend time gabbing with other office workers in the hospital cafeteria. But she always knew what was happening throughout the hospital. At times she could be a wealth of knowledge to help Savannah squelch the rumor mill's propaganda. Internal communication or employee communication handled properly proved to be a valuable asset for the savvy public relations professional. Any corporation or organization as large as the UMMC had a constant bevy of rumors floating about people, jobs, and promotions. When a new project was being discussed, the rumor-mill would run amok. Keeping everyone informed with the correct information from the janitor to the board of directors could be a daunting task. But Savannah knew how to use technology to keep the truth before everyone and squelch the lies that infiltrated the cafeterias and hallways.

She reached for the phone and selected the blinking light.

"Savannah Whitehall," she answered.

"Pendleton, here. I was just informed by Andrew Webster to prepare your husband for discharge on Monday. He is not ready to be discharged and Webster was very secretive about who gave him his orders. What gives?"

"My very wealthy and powerful in-laws," she resigned. "I had no idea of their plans when we talked earlier, but apparently they have decided to move Tom to the Atlanta Medical Center. It supposedly has a better staff and more modern facilities."

"Well, it is an excellent facility, but I doubt it they can do any more than we can. So, it's a done deal?"

"Let me ask you something. As Tom's wife, don't I have the final say for him?"

"Well, I'm not a legal expert, but certainly you should have some voice in the decision making process. This is especially true when a person becomes incapacitated and a relative must act on his behalf. Does Tom have any kind of power of attorney that might address this issue?"

"Not to my knowledge. Shortly after we were married, we talked about having wills drawn up, but never made an appointment with his dad's lawyer."

"I can understand that, with both of you being young. It just isn't a priority. Perhaps you should investigate what might have been established before you married. Anyway, I have my orders and will have Tom ready for travel on Monday. I do feel better knowing he's going to a great rehab and not just home. That was the impression Webster gave."

"I'm checking into other possibilities for keeping Tom here and will let you know what I find out. Thanks for the call."

"Sure. Talk to you later."

"Bye," she said and then hung up.

The spring tornado season was just around the corner and Savannah was reviewing the hospital's disaster response plan. Fixated on the plan she pushed aside the pain surging within her every time she thought about what her mother-in-law was doing. She had a skeleton crisis communication annex to the hospital's plan, but wanted to flesh it out into a more comprehensive document. Crisis communication had been a keen area of interest in college and now she had her own crisis in communicating with her in-laws. They were a formidable force to face with their community influence. With each revision she wrote, her mind moved to how she could apply that communication step or principle to her own situation. The theories of communication weren't just abstract ideas conceived by some college professor, but concepts that related to everyday life. That was what made public relations such a fascinating and dynamic career for her. If she could just get the relations part right with her personal relationships, she would have it made. Someone told her once that, "living in this world isn't hard. It's people that make living difficult." That seemed to be a true axiom for her with her in-laws.

She spent the next two hours writing and rewriting the crisis plan to make sure she had covered all the possible scenarios for her area. The final pages were printing when her cell phone rang.

"Savannah, I don't have good news," her mother began. "I talked with Mr. Brown who made some follow-up calls to the Whitehalls' lawyer. They have covered their bases. Apparently, there is a power of attorney, drafted and signed when Tom was playing football at Southern, that appoints his parents as guardians should he be injured. Since it has never been rescinded, it is still in effect. I'm so sorry, but with that they have the authority to transfer him, if it is in his best interest."

"Oh, Mom. I can't believe it. Barbara has tried to come between Tom and me so many times, and so much as told me that today. This just makes me sick. What can I do?"

"Even if you tried to get an injunction to prevent him from being moved on Monday, a judge would have to later rule in their favor."

"But they aren't. Barbara is doing this to keep him away from me."

"Now, you can't really prove that. And besides, it is one of the best facilities in the nation."

"I know you're right. I'm just . . . ."

"I know, honey. But fighting this right now is not going to help anyone, especially you. Let's just look at some options for you."

"I don't have any."

"Well, why don't you take a few days off and go with them to Atlanta. You can make sure he is settled and meet his doctors."

"Yeah, you're right. You always know the right thing to do. I'll call Andrew and arrange some vacation time. Thanks, Mom."

"You're welcome, honey. Do you want to have dinner with me this evening?"

"Thanks, but I think I'll just go and sit with Tom. I'm not sure I want anything to eat. I'll call you later."

Savannah made her first call to Billy Bob and arranged to meet them at the hospital as Tom was loaded into the ambulance. Her second call was to Webster so she could have the next week off. That meant she needed to finish any hanging projects before she went to visit Tom. She had accrued as much vacation time as possible for a Caribbean cruise for her and Tom to celebrate their anniversary in June. Now she would spend it in Atlanta. But at least she would be with Tom.

Chapter 5

The 45-minute flight from Jackson's International Airport to Atlanta's Hartsfield private jet area had been so frosty that the few words exchanged between Savannah and her in-laws had crackled like icicles hitting the ground. To avoid confrontation Savannah secluded herself in a seat at the rear of the Gulfstream, which had been reconfigured to accommodate Tom's gurney by removing the leather sofa. The nurse took the seat across from Tom's head to monitor his support systems. Barbara and Billy Bob remained up front with the galley separating them from Savannah, Tom and the nurse.

Savannah stared at Tom, but she didn't see the mangled, comatose body. She saw the man who took her to the Painted Lady Seafood Restaurant on the Reservoir just off of Spillway Road on Valentine's Day three years ago.

After college Savannah moved home with her mom to save money and keep her mom company. Her first job as Customer Service Supervisor for South Central Bell did not pay as much as she had hoped to earn. She and Tom began dating on a regular basis as soon as he completed the police academy. They often spoke about marriage in the future, but made no specific plans because Tom wanted to be established in his job first.

With Valentine's Day the next week, Tom was very mysterious about their upcoming date. "I have a surprise for you and I'd like you to wear your powder blue suit and white silk blouse with the wide collar when we go to dinner on Tuesday, okay?"

"Sure, but why?"

"Well, it is one of my favorite outfits because, it makes your grey eyes sparkle like sapphires," he said.

"Anything for you, babe."

The Painted Lady was an upscale restaurant with lavender linen tablecloths and napkins and chairs that were cushioned with pink ladies in horse-racing hats embroidered in the center of a sea-foam green. A grand piano occupied the far corner of the room and most evenings hosted a local concert pianist, who entertained customers with soft melodies. With all its elegance, the seafood was exquisite and reasonably priced. Owned by a local couple who hired college students, they personally trained the entire staff, including the maître d, with impeccable serving techniques. The wife was the head chef and learned her culinary skills in the Tuscany region of Italy. She combined the Mediterranean seasonings of garlic, basil, and oregano with pastas topped by indigenous seafood, thus creating her own delectable delights.

At dinner when the waiter brought their water glasses, Savannah realized that hers didn't lacked ice, but ignored it and ordered, "I'll have the lobster asparagus with penne pasta and a miasta salad, please."

"And I'll have steak and lobster tails with a Caesar salad," added Tom as he handed the waiter their menus.

When the waiter left she turned her attention to her water glass. Gingerly she lifted the glass and realized the coaster was not round, but pink paper folded into fourths.

Tom was desperately trying to be nonchalant, but a grin crept into the corners of his mouth. Resisting the urge to speak, he fidgeted with his napkin and watched his girlfriend's bewildered face as she studied her glass and the paper.

Replacing the glass on the table, Savannah took the pink sheet of paper into both hands and unfolded it. She read:

A Portrait of You

You sit for portraits every night
You know it not. That absent light,
There is a world, in which you live,
Wherein myself to you I give.

You sit for portraits every night.
Near starlight streams in secret sight,
Your face, your eyes are for me alone.
My thoughts of you, my sleep postponed.

You sit for portraits every night.
I know your hair, your lips, your height,
Sweet smells remembered, when I breathe,
I hear your voice, its gentle tease.

You sit for portraits every night.
I dream and dream until it's right.
Until I have you captured fair,
On moonlit canvas I cannot share.

You sit for portraits every night.
You know it not, for it's my plight.
Long after dark, before the dawn,
I lie awake, but you are gone.

You sit for portraits every night.
I long to change this solitary sight,
So I can share with you all my life,
If you will become my very own wife.

Savannah, will you marry me?

Savannah looked up from the poem to see two steel gray eyes fixated on her. Tears welled up in her eyes, her hands became moist, and her heart raced. She wanted to climb across the table and kiss him.

"You are so sweet and so romantic!" she exclaimed. "Yes, I will marry you. I've been waiting years to hear those words from your lips."

"Well, there's one more step to be taken," he almost whispered with his eyes leading her to the water glass.

Following his eyes, she picked up the glass again and looked in. There it was—a small gold ring with a 1.2-carat diamond in a Tiffany setting.

"How am I supposed to get it out—drink the water down to it?"

"No, silly. Here, let me."

He stuck his fork into the glass and pulled the ring out with the tines. After drying it on his napkin, he said, "Your finger, please."

He nervously placed her hand in his left hand and slid the ring onto her finger. Tom knew she was a hopeless romantic and had been sure a diamond was the best Valentine he could give her.

Their salads arrived, but neither had much of an appetite. Throughout the meal, they kept touching their fingertips across the table. Even when the waiter returned to check on the meal, they retracted their hands only briefly. Their conversation was hushed, mostly speaking with their eyes, which were filled with love and ecstatic euphoria. Candlelight from the small taper atop the centerpiece and recessed overhead lighting cast a soft glow on their faces, which radiated their intense emotion. When the last of the entrée had been cleared and they finished their coffee, they strolled outside to the end of the pier in the crisp, February evening. Reflections of the quarter moon danced across the blackness that splashed against the rocks, while stars shimmered above. No clouds blocked their view as they huddled close against the chilly breeze from the water. Tom removed his arm from around her shoulders and turned her to face him. Taking her chin in his hand, he lifted her mouth to his.

"I love you, Savannah Canfield, and I want to be with you for the rest of my life."

"Thomas Whitehall, I love you with all my heart and have loved you since the homecoming dance our senior year. I can't imagine spending my life with anyone but you."

"Then it's settled."

"Wither thou goest, I shall go. And thy people shall be my people."

Those words—which she promised to Tom—echoed in the canyons of her memory. They danced in her head like ghosts taunting her now. It wasn't that she had not meant them with every utterance she spoke, but *his* people did not want her to be *their* people. They were the Whitehalls, owners of the Whitehall Ford dealership in south Jackson, the largest in the city. When the city expanded to the north, the overflow population moved to Brandon and another Whitehall Ford opened just off of Highway 80. At night the lights from the car lot practically welcomed people to Brandon. On Sundays, the *Clarion-Ledger* ran four double truck ads, which also ensured photos in the Lifestyle Section of Barbara and Billy Bob at the reception for opening night at the opera, or the fundraiser for the Junior League, or some other social event.

During Ole Miss's football season, the Whitehalls often hosted post-game parties with only the A-list invitees at River Hills Country Club. Their lives bustled with social events, some promoting worthy causes, but mostly for self-gratification. Money talks and Billy Bob earned enough for him to talk in any circle—political, social, or business. From the Whitehall dormitory at the University of Mississippi to Junior Whitehall's Ford dealerships in Biloxi and Gulfport, the Whitehall name equaled money. To Billy Bob's credit, he had earned most of the money, wheeling and dealing, but his father had been a surgeon at the Baptist Hospital, before it became the Baptist Medical Center. His brother had followed their father's profession and was now Chief of Surgery at BMC. The Whitehall name carried clout wherever or whenever it was used.

Barbara Boyles did not come from money, but from a small town in north Mississippi where her mother raised three children on her own. Her father abandoned her mother when Barbara, the oldest, was eight and her youngest brother was four. Even though she had to help her mother with most of the chores at home, Barbara managed to keep her grades high enough for the honor roll and earned a scholarship to Ole Miss. She had her own struggles, but meeting Billy Bob Whitehall at Ole Miss was a pivotal point for her life.

Savannah shared a similar background which seemed to be a thorn in Barbara's side. No matter how much she wanted to be friends with Barbara, Savannah just didn't measure up to the Whitehall society status. Her father, Bryan Canfield, was a top insurance salesman for Lamar Life, and left a small nest egg that paid off the mortgage and set up college funds for both girls. But his untimely death, when a drunk driver careened into him early one morning on Highway 49, shattered the lives of his girls. No longer could Mary Ann be the happy homemaker, but returned to the workforce to supplement income for basic home maintenance. Without her father for most of her life, Savannah's life had holes that could not be closed. She had to be self-disciplined, tougher and stronger than she wanted to be because her mom couldn't be at home with her. But for her, that was life.

The lesson Mary Ann taught her girls was to learn how to take care of yourself, because life can sometimes hit you with unexpected, cruel blows. From Mary Ann's point of view, she had planned well and lived well. Loosing Bryan had been a cruel blow and now Tom's accident seemed to be a sucker punch to her small family.

Barbara blamed Savannah for it, because her mother-in-law was convinced that Tom didn't play pro football or join the Whitehall Ford team because his wife supported his decision to be a policeman—a word that sounded like an insult when his mother spoke it. According to her it had to be Savannah's influence that prevented Tom from following the path laid out for him—one for success and opulence.

On the other hand, Savannah knew that being assigned to SWAT was a dream for Tom and she wanted him to fulfill his dream. With his degree in criminology Tom was on the fast track to detective when he was asked to join SWAT. This elite squad trained harder than any other unit and earned national recognition for Jackson's police department. They took down a major drug ring in South Jackson that recruited high school kids to sell the drugs to other students. It was a major coup with Tom as a key player and earned special recognition from the chief.

For them life was great. After she snagged the position of Director of Communications by being available with the right credentials at the right time, she knew she broke new ground as a department head at a prestigious hospital, especially for a woman who was not a doctor.

The hospital was desperate to fill the vacancy abruptly created when the previous director moved to California, but couldn't match the salary requirements for most of the applicants. The salary offer for Savannah was a small pay cut, but her experience level—especially the college internships—made her the top replacement choice for the plum position. She supervised a staff of five and managed the hospital's volunteer program, which included a hundred volunteers on any given day. It was obvious she loved the work, even though the demands could range from announcing breakthrough research to dealing with the death of trauma victims in the emergency unit. She successfully juggled the good news and bad news stories generated by a major hospital and the people associated with it. Her work was exciting, demanding, and rewarding—but more than anything she did at work, despite what her mother-in-law thought, she was devoted Tom.

Every day was a new adventure that could range from boredom to moments of sheer terror. Neither of them knew from one day to the next what unforeseeable exploit would greet them. They had friends, like the Thorntons and some of the married guys on the force, with whom they socialized, but these occasions were limited by crazy work schedules. However, friends became scarce now that Tom's and her life were turned upside down. Except for visits by Chris and Pat, only family members viewed the comatose vegetable with tubes coming out of his nostrils, a respirator pumping air into lifeless lungs. In a way she was glad because this was not her Tom. It was a shell of the man she knew. He was a vibrant, energetic person, full of life, and a joy for living. Maybe Barbara was right in bringing him to Atlanta. Maybe there was hope at this facility. That's what Savannah had—*hope*.

Hope comes from many sources. For some, it is the intangible concept that makes them preserver through hardships and self-denial to reach a goal. The hope for freedom has kept prisoners of war alive through unbelievable torture. Hope for a prize kept Olympic athletes training, when they were physically spent. Savannah had hope, because she had character—a character filled by the love God's Spirit poured into her heart. Sitting beside Tom as she prayed for him, Savannah recalled a scripture from *Romans 5* she had memorized as a teenager:

> *And we rejoice in the hope of the glory of God.*
> *Not only so, but we also rejoice in our sufferings,*
> *because we know that suffering produces*

perseverance; perseverance, character; and character, hope. And hope does not disappoint us, because God has poured out His love into our hearts by the Holy Spirit, whom he has given us.

She did not know what pitfalls or pebbles were imbedded in the road ahead, but she knew she had hope, for her and for Tom, and for the future.

Chapter 6

"**A**re you still here?"

The question startled Savannah, who turned to see her mother-in-law coming through the door of Tom's private room at the end of the corridor. Although there was a brocade recliner positioned within eye level of a window overlooking the grassy hill below, Savannah chose the moderately cushioned straight-back chair, so she could keep her hand on Tom's. She had been mesmerized by the dull hum and gurgle of the lifesaving machines on the other side of the bed. Hanging metal rods and mechanical apparatuses against the stark white bed sheets and blanket drowned out any semblance of softness that the wall of flowers and comfortable chairs were supposed to provide.

Her mind transported her to when he was at the police academy. He seemed so far away from her and they didn't talk much. Once in a while he would find time to write her a letter. She stroked his hand and remembered one of his letters:

We certainly have a different perspective on life here. We expect the worst in people, plan for the most violent and have little hope for the best. Pat, one of the other cadets, calls the instructors names like "peanut brain" and "idiot" under his breath. I'm afraid they are going to hear him and not know who said it. They are just doing their job, but he refers to them as less than human. I tried to explain to him that this is just a training environment and they have to get us ready to face a very cruel world. I think my words fell on deaf ears. Pat is such a risk taker, living on the edge everyday. Please pray for Pat and the rest of us so we all make it home safely. I know you pray for me, because I can feel the power of your prayers.

All my love,
Tom

His letters were never long, but always poignant with his concern for others. Savannah memorized most of them because she read and reread them several times a day. She wrote back words of encouragement for Tom. Sometimes she would include something funny that happened at work or that her mother said. If she had a problem though, she turned to her mom rather than writing to Tom about it. She thought he had enough to worry about without her minor setbacks at South Central Bell. Her life was pretty simple then.

There were no tears streaming down her face, but inside Savannah cried a thousand tears. Tom was a beautiful gift from God. Unfortunately, Barbara Whitehall's eyes were clouded by plastic judgments and she never saw the love shared by her son and his wife.

"Yes, ma'am. I am," were her barely audible words.

"How long do you plan to stay?" came a terse query and glaring eyes.

"I want to be by Tom's side until he regains consciousness or until I have used the last day of my vacation and sick leave."

"I just meant for today. How long are you going to be here?"

"I've made arrangements to sleep in the recliner. I can use the bathroom to freshen up. Besides, I really don't have anywhere else to go. This is where I want to be anyway. Really, Barbara, I just plan to stay with Tom as long as I can."

"I see. Well, Billy Bob and I will just fly back to Jackson tonight. There's no sense in us staying at a hotel waiting for you to leave," she said glancing around the room as if surveying it to redecorate the austere setting. Barbara liked putting her decorative flair on everything she touched.

"Barbara, you don't have to do that. I don't want to keep you from seeing your son. I just want to be near him. I want to be here when he wakes up and I know he will."

"Like I said, his father and I will simply fly back to Jackson and return when you leave."

"You know all the tests will be finished this week and we should have the results by next week."

"What's that got to do with anything?"

"Well, won't you be transferring him back to Jackson, so we can all be closer to him?"

"That's not the plan."

"What do you mean?"

"I mean, that we have arranged for him to stay as long as he is incapacitated."

"But, why? I know this is a great facility, but so is the Med Center in Jackson."

"This is the best rehab in the South and that's where my baby boy will be. And when you leave here, I'll be back to take care of him."

"Suit yourself. I will let you know when that happens," Savannah retorted as she was no longer able to keep her emotions under control. She was surprised at her outburst and evidently Barbara was taken aback, too.

"Fine," she demurred. "Just let me know if there is any change in him."

"Yes ma'am, I will," she replied more curtly than she expected.

Barbara spun around, burst out the door, letting it slam behind her.

Once Barbara was out of sight, Savannah's dam burst and the tears gushed down her cheeks. The salt stung her face, but her outburst was more from anger than sadness. It infuriated her that Barbara was so heartless, not just to her but also toward Tom. Just because she was here didn't mean his parents couldn't visit him. Trembling with anger, Savannah struggled to compose herself. She couldn't believe how edgy she was.

"Oh God, please help me to love Barbara and to honor and respect her as a person, and especially as Tom's mother," she prayed aloud. Gently she patted Tom's hand before she went to the bathroom to rinse away the mascara streaks beneath her eyes. What she had spoken was between her and God. She didn't want anyone else to know the struggle she had with Barbara.

Her phone rang just as she turned off the water at the lavatory.

"This is Savannah," she answered, without not able to read the incoming call number through clouded eyes.

"Hi honey, I just called to see how Tom's doing."

"Mom, I'm so glad you called. Tom is the same, still in a coma. They have a very aggressive physical therapy program to keep his muscles from atrophy. But all of the brain wave tests have shown no improvement."

"How long will all the tests take?"

"By next week we will have the results of all the tests, but I think Barbara plans to keep him here indefinitely."

"But why? Wouldn't it be better if he were back in Jackson?"

"That's what I thought, but apparently, that's not the Whitehall way. She is waiting for me to leave and then will come back here to stay with Tom. Or so she says."

"Is she going to take shifts with you?"

"No, Mom. She is flying back to Jackson and won't come back until I go home."

"That woman never ceases to amaze me! I know you must be upset about this."

"Mom, has Mr. Brown been able to find any way that I can have Tom transferred back to UMMC? I should have rights as his wife, shouldn't I?"

"He's still looking into it, but it will take a judge rescinding that power of attorney for the Whitehalls to do it. And you know that Mr. Whitehall knows all the judges personally. The other problem is Mr. Brown's recent case load. He's doing this pro bono and it just hasn't been his priority. He really thinks legally it is a losing battle."

"Couldn't you persuade him to move it up on his priority list?"

"I will see what I can do, honey."

"Thanks, Mom. You're the best. You have the uncanny ability to be there for me when I need you. Does God always tell you when to call me?"

"Yes, He does. I was just praying for you and knew that you needed me."

"You always do."

"That's what mothers are for."

"Thanks, Mom. I love you."

"I love you, too, honey. Are you staying at a hotel or at the hospital?"

"I'll stay here in Tom's room. It's really a suite with a sitting area, private bath, and settee where I can sleep. The hospital cafeteria is open 24 hours, so I can eat whenever I need to."

"Just get some rest. I don't want you to wear yourself out."

"I will. But, Mom, I only have two weeks of vacation and a few days of sick leave accrued. I haven't been at the hospital long enough to have extended time off. Andrew explained that to me before I came. So without longevity, I just have to use accrued time. I just pray that it will be enough so both of us will go home."

"I hope so, honey," Mary Ann tried to be cheerful. "Well, if you need me, just call."

"I will. And thanks again for the phone call."

"Certainly, honey. Bye."

"Bye, Mom."

She felt better already and said a prayer of thanks for God giving her a mom who always knew when she needed her. Maybe she wasn't there physically, but emotionally she was and their lines of communication were always open. Facing an uphill battle with the Whitehalls and the uncertainty of Tom's condition, she could be thankful for her mom.

At the same time Savannah received a call from her mother, Barbara received one from Mitch Adams, a private investigator from Jackson.

"Mrs. Whitehall, I think you'll be interested in what I found concerning your son's accident."

"That's what my husband is paying you for. Do tell me."

"I would prefer showing it to you in person. When will you be back in Jackson?"

"We are packing the car as we speak and should be back in Jackson within two hours. Why don't you meet us at the house at 7 p.m.?"

"I'll do that, ma'am. See you at seven."

Chapter 7

Savannah managed to stretch her two weeks of vacation and four days of sick leave into three weeks. But Tom remained the same. No worse and no better. He was still hooked up to tubes, a respirator, and traction bars, creating a spectral network of artificial life.

When Georgia Kane came to bathe Tom, Savannah helped. It took both of them to lift and turn Tom and their teamwork led to a quick friendship. Born in a rural town of the state, whose name she bore, Georgia loved being a nurse and it showed in every task she undertook.

"I've seen you reading your Bible to him," commented Georgia during one of the daily rituals. "I know that must mean a lot to him, hearing those words from the good Lord."

"I just know they comfort me, Georgia. I don't know if Tom can hear them or not, but if he does, they are the best words to hear."

"Ready to turn him?" Georgia asked as she placed her arms under Tom.

"Um hum," she replied straining to pull Tom's shoulders toward her.

"On three. One, two, three. There we go."

"I couldn't do this by myself."

"It's really my job, but I appreciate your help," said Georgia as she began sponging Tom's now pale skin. "I know you want to make sure we take good care of him for you, but you're here every day. Don't you ever go home?"

"I will be going back to Jackson soon. So every minute I can, I want to spend it with Tom."

"I see. You can be here as much as you want. Would you like me to bring you dinner before I leave at the end of my shift?"

"That's very sweet of you, Georgia. But I do go down to the Canteen to grab something and I drink the water the aides bring in the pitchers."

"If you don't mind me asking, what happened to his mother? She was here and telling everyone what to do. Then, poof, she was gone."

"It's really a long story, but the short of it is that she will be back when I leave."

"Are you like taking turns with sitting with Mr. Whitehall?"

"Not exactly. She is waiting for me to leave before she comes back. She knows I have to get back to work and she's not happy about that."

"I guess she never had to work or she never approved of you."

"You guessed right on both counts. And she resents the fact that I have a job and am not at home having her grandbabies. I've never quite figured her out. I know she begrudges Tom's marrying me because my family was not the elite of Jackson. And I think she had someone picked out for him, but it wasn't me."

"Umm hum. She did seem to be a lady in charge of everything."

"That's about the size of it. You ready to roll him to the other side?" asked Savannah when Georgia moved the tray with the pan of water to the other side.

"Yes. Ready? Turn," she said as they turned Tom up on his other side. "I don't suppose she'll be helping with this kind of thing."

"No, I imagine she'll be supervising it."

"I see. Do you think she'll be here all day?"

"I really can't tell you for sure. She'll likely have shopping trips and other things to occupy her time. However, she's a devoted mother. Sometimes a little too devoted."

"Umm hum. I know what you mean."

"Listen, Georgia, do you think you could keep me informed when I go back? I work at the University of Mississippi Medical Center and could give you a toll-free number or you can call my cell, which would be even better."

"I'm sure we can arrange something, but won't your mother-in-law keep you informed?"

"She might give me periodic updates, but I want to know any changes and get a daily report."

"Well, between Esther and me, we should be able to keep you well advised on his condition."

"That would be great. Are you about finished?"

"Yes. I just need to check all his tubes. Did he do his PT yet?"

"No, they usually come in between 10 and 11 for that."

Georgia breezed out of the room as quietly as she had entered. Her job was done for now and she wanted to leave the lonely, young lady with her husband. In her years of working at the hospital, the floor nurse knew when she was needed and when she wasn't. Savannah needed a friend and she would be that friend. She kept up with Tom's unchanging condition for the three weeks Savannah sat by his side. Some days she would hear a soft soprano melody wafting from the room. Other days it was words being read from the Bible or another book. Or maybe it was just hearing someone talking in low tones. But Georgia knew Savannah was there speaking to her beloved, letting him know someone was watching and caring for him.

The day Savannah dreaded finally arrived. She took one last look at him before leaving. As much as she wanted to take him back to Jackson with her, she knew it would be an insurmountable task, because no one said, "No," to Barbara Whitehall—and so far, Mr. Brown had found no legal way to rescind the power of attorney Barbara held.

At least he's getting excellent care; she thought and resigned herself to accepting the situation. She knew she had spent 24/7 of the last three weeks, which was more than they normally shared at home, with him and hoped that somehow, somewhere in his subconscious he heard what she said.

"My darling, I don't want you to forget my voice. I want you to hear it in your head when I am not here. Don't forget how much I love you," she spoke into his ear.

She must have said she loved him a hundred times a day. She knew there were reports of people being able to recall events that occurred during their unconscious states and she wanted every millisecond she had with him to count. If her voice could penetrate his comatose state, she wanted him to hear her heart and connect with him as they had before his accident.

Taking Delta's last flight for the evening from Hartsfield to JIA was uneventful, but expensive for a one-way ticket. There was no company jet available for her—just the overbooked cattle-car of a Boeing 727. By the time the taxi dropped her at the front door, she was exhausted. She managed to carry her one suitcase up the stairs, through the first door on the left, and deposited it beside the Southern pine chest before she kicked her shoes into the walk-in closet. She was tempted to do what her mother had scolded her for—to dive head first into the inviting softness of Winslow antique pine bed and have a good cry. After all, she deserved it.

Just looking at the sapphire and lilac circles inlaid with multicolored triangles of the hand-made double-ring patchwork quilt draped across the king-size bed, reminded her of the hours her mother worked piecing together scraps from many of Savannah's childhood dresses. It was a very special wedding gift and like most mementos, it was to be treated gently—not to be misused. When she and Tom moved into their townhouse, the quilt with its hunter green background with multi-colored rings joined by triangles became the focal point for decorating the bedroom. The custom-made Tiffany chintz drapes in sapphire, framed by the rich, hunter green lining and trumpet valance, encased the picture window, which faced east and overlooked the Reservoir. Her hope chest in antique pine was centered under the window. She found a collection of four Italian prints in greens, blues, and lilac and framed them in pine to offset the eggshell walls. Her sister had embroidered royal blue irises with yellow stamens, long jade stems, and basil leaves on doilies for the dresser top and nightstands. But her mother's quilt captured her eyes with its beauty and represented the stalwart of strength to do the right thing. She needed rest for the night to meet the hectic demands of public relations tomorrow.

Daily, and sometimes more frequently, phones calls from Wanda had helped her to stay on top of key events—fortunately nothing earth shattering had occurred. Wanda's exceptional administrative acumen allowed her to run the office via long-distance, even faxing essential documents to the Atlanta hospital. Life went on for others; it was for Tom that time stood still and in some vicarious way for Savannah's heart, too. While she knew that as long as Tom was on life-support, there was still hope for him to recover, the loss of his companionship struck a chord deep in her sub-consciousness. Her heart ached for him as did the rest of her being. She was missing half of herself and that made everything difficult. Even though she had to focus her attention on other matters, her heart remained in hundreds of miles away in a hospital room.

Arriving at the office around six allowed Savannah to get a jump on the day. She breezed down the tiled hallway past the empty and dimly lit administrative offices. The elevator stood open at the end of the first floor, waiting to deposit her at the barely carpeted rooms on the eighth floor. Rounding the corner to her department's suite of offices she slowed her pace. She fidgeted with her keys to open the door, took a deep breath, and stepped in. Everything looked the same as it had three weeks ago. The schefflera tree graced the corner with tri-pronged, lime-colored almonds overhanging the midnight blue sofa chair. Wanda's corn plant was wedged between her file box and the telephone on the mahogany veneer desk. Her armless swivel chair was securely tucked under her computer on the citizen L desk. A box of tissues held its place to the right of the printer and an old family photograph faced the middle of the calendar blotter centered on the main surface. Three mahogany file cabinets lined the wall behind her desk with a small faux mahogany bookcase and lamp table stationed on the other side of the door to Savannah's office. Only the essentials were in view with all being well-organized. The dark veneers warmed the coldness of the grey divan with its deep blue obtuse triangles.

Savannah plopped her leather briefcase down on her executive desk and noticed that the Boston fern hanging by the window and the two butterfly palms beyond the conference table looked very healthy. Considering the hours she often spent here, she was grateful for such a bright, efficient office. The philodendron on her desk had grown and cascaded down to the floor. Wanda had insisted that the office have real plants, not the plastic ones in the other offices. She was right. They presented a friendlier atmosphere and enhanced the drabness of a sterile environment.

She took her jacket off and hung it on the hall tree in the corner of the room before positioning her chair at her desk where she could easily peruse the stack of papers Wanda had neatly prioritized for her. It was early May and she was beginning to receive volunteer applications for the summer. Without her ginning up special events, and with the annual Spring Fling charity ball in early April, the next scheduled event was months away. This gave her time to finish her crisis communications plans, schedule a drill, and be ready for the next emergency. She had breathing room. And she could monitor Tom's condition with the help of Georgia Kane and Esther Evans at the Atlanta Rehab Center.

UMMC was primarily established as a teaching hospital, but that included research as well. Andrew Webster's keen judgment of character enabled him to recruit some of the best specialists as department heads for the hospital. These men and women were not only favorably esteemed in their fields, but were also abundantly skilled managers. Webster made sure his hospital team was trained so he could do his job of managing the finances, hiring and firing personnel, and ensuring the functionality of the organization. Raising money for extensive research projects, building additions, and modernizing equipment was a responsibility that Andrew and Savannah shared. Two major events combined with several mini concerts as well as the state and federal funds contributed to the annual budget. Planning for the fall festival began the day after the spring fling.

In reviewing the folder Wanda marked "hot," she found the results of several tests conducted by the rehabilitation center that provided break-through technology for paralysis. This would merit a press conference, which would mean a multitude of calls to make it worthwhile. She always had to stay one jump ahead and planning was the key to a successful program. Appropriate leaks and tweets lured a wide range of media interest from local coverage to trade publications.

She could handle the last-minute problems that would crop up and wreak havoc with her day, but she much preferred the planned events that she meticulously engineered, and observed as they unfolded with the precision of a well-oiled machine. A strategist, Savannah began organizing the press conference for Wednesday by outlining the event—the time of day was critical to ensure maximum media coverage—even with 24-hour coverage, the bulk of the media still had regular news times. Using the foyer in front of the rehab center with the hospital's logo and name behind it would be the perfect visual backdrop and allow the doctors to enter from the doors to the right of the logo. She would emcee the event and begin with Dr. Richard Roddenburg, the head of the rehab center. He would make a statement, authored by her as well as a hospital fact sheet.

By the time Wanda arrived, the Director of Communications had outlined the events, selected the media to notify, drafted a memo to the rehab center with the proposal to be attached, and written the opening statements. Later in the day she and Doug, the media specialist, worked on proposed questions for the center to answer before the event. By developing a list of responses to what could be difficult or embarrassing questions prior to the press conference; she could put the researchers at ease in front of the media and prevent an awkward situation. It was also one of the ways she could convince a group of introverted scientists to tell their story—otherwise they would hide in the bowels of the laboratory never to be seen. It was opportunities like this that made her job fun and contributed to the steady influx of capital that put the hospital on the leading edge of medicine in the South.

Wednesday rolled around without a hitch and Dr. Roddenburg was a star. He looked good, spoke well, and made the hospital shine. All the prep time Savannah and Doug spent with the researcher paid off in aces. The media loved him and his answers even to speculative questions were so positive that Andrew thought he was a PR pro.

Rain violently struck like pellets against the panes of her window as the eerie avocado-gray light flooded the room. It was late Friday afternoon bringing an end to a very busy first week back for Savannah. Wanda left early to do some shopping as a "job well-done" appreciation for handling so much while Savannah was away. She heard Doug, the last one of her staff, shutting down his computer and getting ready to leave.

"This has been some week, Mrs. Whitehall," the lean, dark-haired young man said with his back against the door jam and hands in his pockets. In building her team, Savannah hired Doug as an intern last summer and when he finished his degree in December, she offered him a permanent job. He had potential and talent, two particular skills Savannah was looking for. During his internship he had proven to be a go-getter with integrity, an ingredient hard to find in this business.

"Yes, but quite successful, don't you think?"

"If you mean the press conference, absolutely!"

"Well, it was the highlight of the week, for sure. But since Wednesday we have managed to complete our crisis plan, thanks to your work on it."

"Yes ma'am, but do you think everyone will buy off on it?"

"I have no doubt that they will. You see each event that we complete successfully like the press conference builds confidence in our staff—you know ROI, return on investment. It puts money in the till, a significant way to measure our success!"

"I like the way you think," Doug's words bellowed across the room when the pounding against the window abruptly stopped.

Startled by the silence, they turned to look outside. Spring storms were normal weather patterns across central Mississippi and kept the hills and valleys verdant. But, when the sky transformed to an olive-gray, be warned! No longer did the clouds bring a refreshing spring rain, but they were ominous. Savannah pushed back her chair and started towards the window as Doug moved slowly from the doorway.

"Look! There's a funnel cloud," she pointed to the western sky where a dark gray whirling mass rotated with a wide tail dipping down, bouncing beneath the menacing heavens.

"It's heading right towards us."

"No, I think it is further west than we are," she corrected his assumption.

For several minutes they scanned the clouds for other funnels, but a wave of blackness with the return of the pounding rain prevented them for seeing any more. The chime of the telephone redirected their attention to her desk. Picking up the receiver, she answered, "Communications Director, may I help you?"

"Mrs. Whitehall, this is Miriam Weeks in ER. We have a situation here. A tornado hit North Park Mall just a few minutes ago and we are expecting casualties any minute. We've sent all our ambulance crews. Can you come down here?"

"Certainly, Miriam. Doug and I will be right there."

"Great! We can use all the hands available."

Savannah hung up the phone and turned to Doug, "I hope you don't have any immediate plans, because we are needed in ER stat. Grab your keys and let's go. I'll explain on the way."

Taking her keys out of the desk drawer, she locked her desk, then her office door and the outer door before they headed toward the elevator that Doug had summoned.

When they arrived, the ER was nearly empty, but a multitude of voices were coming across the radio receiver for the ambulance teams. Moaning and groaning could be heard in the background and people yelling commands. The phone at the nurse's station was ringing incessantly. Without waiting to be told Savannah and Doug began answering the telephones. The first rule in a crisis is to do no harm, which also equated to taking care of people's needs first. They were not medically qualified, but by taking on administrative duties, they allowed those with the right expertise to better use their time.

"It will be only minutes before the first casualties arrive," Miriam announced as doctors and nurses began converging near the nurse's station and Miriam barked out their assignments. "We have to be ready."

As soon as the ambulances began arriving, it may have appeared to be mayhem to an outsider, but with Miriam in charge, the ER operated efficiently as each victim moved through triage to treatment. People lay on gurneys in the hallway as the most seriously injured were rolled down to surgery. Savannah and Doug processed paperwork, helped those with minor injuries to find a place to wait, met family members, answered phones and made calls to families of those they had identified. Only one reporter from the *Clarion-Ledger* came to the medical center. Most of the media were dispatched to the mall where the tornado ripped through the line of stores, including the Jitney-Jungle grocery store filled with Friday evening shoppers.

> *"Emergency teams are here still working to rescue some of the people trapped when the walls and the roof of the Jitney-Jungle collapsed in the wake of the tornado,"* stated Dee Dee Dempsey, the reporter for WLBT, the NBC affiliate, from the television mounted on the wall across from the waiting lounge.
>
> *"The police estimated that from one to two hundred people were at North Park this evening when it struck. Many have already been taken to every hospital in the area. We expect to get a confirmation of the number killed later, but the police have indicated that however high the number is, it is expected to climb as the evening wears on."*

The news continued with more pictures of injured and rescuers digging through debris to find casualties.

"It looks like we will be getting more patients," said Savannah looking across the room to the television set.

"I don't know where we'll put them," replied Doug as he shuffled more papers, trying to keep them organized.

"Well, don't worry! Miriam does! Our problem will come when the media move from the shopping center to the hospitals to cover the carnage. We'll be here for quite some time; do you need to let someone know you're still here?"

"Not really. I didn't have plans this evening anyway."

"I just thought you might call before the next wave of casualties . . ." but before she could finish the sentence, the doors burst open as EMTs pushed more gurneys into the crammed reception area. Two secretaries from the front offices were assisting in paperwork management, but keeping up with those being brought in was insurmountable.

By midnight the ER had finally moved the last of its tornado victims to other parts of the hospital for follow-up evaluations. One of the secretaries had created a list from the piles of admittance sheets with 92 names. Miriam dismissed the administrative help and Savannah sent Doug home. The two sat down behind the counter separating the nurse's station from the rest of the reception area.

"Tomorrow's going to be just as busy," began Savannah as she sipped on some freshly brewed coffee.

"Yes, but the storm is over. Now we focus on alleviating pain and restoring those who were traumatized."

"I'm sure the media will be here in force to get updates on the people. I should call them with the numbers we have. What's the latest on the ones that were brought here either DOA or have died?"

"Let me see. Umm. Of the 92 we received, four were DOA and we had one die in surgery. We have 26 in ICU. I called four nurses who were off-duty to supplement ICU's staff," Miriam mumbled as she flipped through the forms collected on a clipboard. "Okay, that leaves 61 who have been admitted with various injuries that were not life-threatening. Looks like most of them have contusions and lacerations that have been treated initially but need additional treatment. I'm not sure where all these people are. We didn't have that many empty beds."

"What about those on the critical list? Do you have numbers for me?"

"They will probably change overnight. Are you going to call now or in the morning?"

"Well, I won't make any calls until morning, but if I get calls before I can get to the hospital, I could use these numbers," said the PR director, knowing how many media had her cell number.

"I see. Well, as of now, we have 16 of those in critical condition and six in serious condition and the other four require ICU to continuously monitor them. Will that help?"

"That's perfect. Do you know if any of them are high profile names?"

"I'd have to run down the entire list, but off-hand, I'd say I can't remember any particular names."

"Well, we need to make sure everyone's next of kin has been notified. I wouldn't release the names now, but just want to be ready for the media. Thanks for your help, Miriam. Now I can go home, get a shower, some rest and do it all again in the morning. How 'bout you?"

"Now that Martha Ranker is here, I'll let her take over. She came in early around 10, but it was so crazy."

"I know. But personally, I'm glad you were here when it all started. You are one tough cookie when the chips are down and you get the job done."

"You're not so bad yourself, young lady. This has been no picnic for you and you've pitched in to do whatever. This hospital is lucky to have Miss PR around."

"Well, now that we have established our mutual admiration club, shall we leave?"

"I'm ready. Where's you car parked?"

"I'm in the back parking lot," said Savannah thinking about the reserved spot that was a perk of her position. "What about yours?"

"I'm in the garage."

"Why don't we walk to my car and I'll give you a ride to yours?" Savannah asked as she thought how sinister the garage could be even though it was well-lit.

"Sounds like a deal to me," Miriam agreed and grabbed her purse and tote bag from her desk drawer. The cadence of Savannah's heels echoed down the hall while Miriam's oxfords squished softly as the two women chatted their way through the fluorescent-lighted halls leading to the back of the complex.

Even through the pouring rain, the hospital's security lights made it look like a fortress perched majestically at the crest of one of Jackson's many hills like the castles on the Rhine. But instead of cool, sparkling water flowing gently below its turrets, UMMC was encircled by hot, black asphalt perhaps like the lava that once flowed from the spewing volcano, which sat dormant 2,900 feet below the downtown area near the coliseum.

The gated parking lot, reserved 24-hours a day for key hospital staff, was located at the back of the hospital to preserve the beauty of the perfectly manicured field of emerald dotted with majestic southern pines and oaks. Tanzanite and tourmaline hydrangeas lined the west side of the building and a row of Mr. Lincoln roses bordered the east side, with junipers rising behind them in lush spires that were nearly blue. The flat roof and box-shaped, concrete wings of the building loomed above Woodrow Wilson Drive as a stalwart of healing.

Chapter 8

A s she twisted the faucets to the off position the cascading waterfall dried up and Savannah heard her phone ringing. Wrapping the terry-cloth turban around her head to soak up drippings from her long, golden flax, she clothed her body in a sheet towel before running to catch the phone by her bed.

"This is Savannah."

"Oh, hi, Dee Dee," she said plopping down on the edge of her still unmade bed. The foam-green LED numbers displayed 6:37 a.m., but Dee Dee and she had a personal history dating back to their college days. Although both had the same degrees in journalism from USM, their career paths departed with Dee Dee in the role of reporter and Savannah as a public relations practitioner. Both had landed jobs in Jackson and periodically met for lunch to discuss their careers. This morning Dee Dee called her friend to get the scoop on the tornado victims.

"Yes, I have the numbers as of last night. But you know we can't give you names yet."

"But what about prominent community leaders?"

"Yes, I can check for any key people. I sort of checked last night, but didn't see any significant names."

"So, are the numbers on the record?"

"Sure you can quote me on the numbers. That's not a problem. Just make sure that you qualify them as being from last night. I'm getting ready to go in now, so I'll check the status and give you a call in, say, an hour. Where can I reach you?

"Just call my cell."

"Okay, I'll talk to you then. Bye."

They understood deadlines and were task-oriented people, which had been one of the reasons for their close personal and professional friendship. Dee Dee became the youngest anchorwoman for the evening news in the state because she had brains, talent and knockout looks. She wasn't just a pretty talking head, she had the wherewithal to gather, interpret, and report the news. When she needed news from the medical community, she called her friend Savannah. She wasn't her only source, but she was always in the know about all the hospitals and their staffs. It was her job to know.

Fully dressed for work, she opened the bedroom drapes noticing that the morning emerged fresh and new with the sun's rays striking the swollen reservoir's ridge. It was hard to imagine the angry waves crashing against the rocks lining the west bank of the manmade lake. The Ross Barnett Reservoir spanned 33,000 acres, which appeared calm and serene now, was completed in 1963. Named for the 52nd governor of the state, the landmark served as a major water source and recreational facility with a 10-gate spillway. More than 4,600 homes surrounded the magnificent outdoor recreation area, placing Tom and Savannah's townhouse on prime real estate.

The tornado's path left a swathe of litter from the shopping center and neighborhood homes, but none of that was visible from Savannah's window. The fierce lightning that accompanied last night's thundering twister was nowhere to be found as she enjoyed the beauty of God's rays dancing across sparkling diamonds swishing to and fro. She remembered the verse from the 30th Psalm that said, "weeping may remain for the night, but rejoicing comes in the morning." However, she wasn't sure how much rejoicing there would be for the families of those in the hospital and those who didn't make it. She wished they had all been Christians, but had her doubts. Perhaps the ones who had made it were given a second chance.

Turning away she picked up her handbag and headed for the stairs. She had a job to do. The hospital needed her expertise today and that was where she was going. Like the patients' families, she carried a heavy heart, longing for someone with whom she could not communicate—her Tom. Pushing her emotions aside, she slung her purse onto her shoulder and snatched her keys from the hook by the back door.

Traffic was light before 7:30 allowing Savannah an early arrival at the back of the hospital. She hurried down the stairs down to the morgue, picked up the casualty list, and then took the elevator to the main floor. Her pumps pounded the sandstone hallway, which led to the set of elevators for the hospital's business offices. From the morgue's list and the updated list of tornado victims in the hospital, she could prepare her statement to the press. Looking over the names for any high profile victims, she made a mental note to double check that their next of kin had been notified. It would be unthinkable to release someone's name and have the family members learn of a death from the TV or radio.

She turned the key in the lock to her office and flipped the light switch. Her eyes fixated on a name she recognized. Stunned, she dropped into her chair with such force that it rolled backwards off the Plexiglas and onto the carpet. How could she have not seen this person being brought in last night? Tears welled up in her eyes blurring her vision as she stared at the paper rattling between her trembling fingers.

"No!" she told herself as she threw the paper down and pulled her chair back to the desk. She had work to do and refused to allow her own tragedy to cloud her ability to represent the hospital during a time of crisis. "Momma always said, 'put others first,' and that's what I have to do," she chided.

She reviewed the list again. No other names grabbed her attention. Pulling out a notepad and pen, she wrote out her press statement.

> *After the tornado hit North Park Mall yesterday, the University of Mississippi Medical Center received 92 patients. Regrettably eight of them died, either before arriving here or since then of injuries sustained as a result of the tornado's devastation. We have confirmed that their next of kin have been notified and will provide you with a list of the deceased. However, it is not our policy to release a list of current patients and that information is not available. The hospital's surgical team, the Intensive Care Unit, and all off-duty medical and technical staff worked*

tirelessly to save as many lives as possible. With an increase of 84 patients, our experienced and highly skilled staff will continue to provide the best care available for these people in a facility built to meet this challenge. Our hospital and staff are here to ensure the healing process and return them to their families.

I will now take questions.

She tore the page from her notebook and placed it in the center of her desk. She wished Wanda were here to type it for her, but quickly put that thought aside. She reached for the receiver and punched Dee Dee's number.

"This is Dee Dee," she sharply replied after two rings.

"Hi, Dee Dee. Savannah here. I have the list of names. There's no high profile name listed. Do you want me to fax it to your office?"

"Thanks, but that won't be necessary. Apparently, the mayor's wife was one of those shoppers last night. She was taken to St. Dominic's and has been released."

"Oh, I hadn't heard. Guess I've been caught up with things here. Thanks for the info."

"You're welcome. Well, gotta go. Talk to you soon."

"Sure, bye."

Savannah wanted to talk to Dee Dee. In reality, she just needed someone to talk to. But now was not the time. She glared at the list of deceased as if it were the culprit. Her thoughts were interrupted.

"Good morning!" came a cherry greeting from Doug.

Looking up and pasting a smile on her face Savannah replied, "And a good morning to you. You look like you're ready to tackle the day."

"I am here to work, ma'am."

"Well, good because we have lots to do. But first, I have to show you the list of victims."

Doug came over to her desk and picked up the list from the morgue. There was the name Savannah had highlighted—Wanda Crutchfield. "Oh, my God!" he cried.

"I know. I couldn't believe it myself. I didn't even see her name last night."

"What are we going to do without her?"

"I don't know. I can't imagine functioning in this office without Wanda. She was here when I came and taught me so much about the hospital."

"Have you talked to her family?" he asked, returning the list to his boss' desk.

"I think she has a married brother who lives in California. It indicates here that he was notified by the hospital's chaplain last night. Other than that, I guess we were her family."

The two PR professionals busied themselves for the next few hours by arranging a press conference in the hospital's front foyer for 10 a.m. and making dozens of phone calls. They hardly spoke, only needing brief confirmations of appropriate preparations. Regardless of the crisis, their responses were well-rehearsed and automatic.

Chapter 9

Sunday morning Savannah pulled the drapes allowing the fresh light to flood the dining room and streak across the sand and brownstone plush carpet in the living room. On most days such brilliance would make her face radiate, but not today. Her heart was so cold with her concern for those she loved and cared about, that she simply turned and walked away without enjoying the exhilarating warmth. She had purposely slept late, not wanting to attend the couples Sunday school class by herself, but forcing herself to meet her mother for the worship service.

She found her mother on her usual pew, the third from the front on the right hand side of the sanctuary and slipped in beside her smiling and nodding silent greetings to those around. It was expected to be pleasant and cheerful in church and she obliged. Up in the balcony she saw the Whitehalls perched in the center section in front of the television camera—the service was broadcast live every Sunday morning on WLBT. She managed to maintain her pleasant pretense throughout the singing, the greeting time, and the special music, a beautiful solo by Mrs. Susan Evans, who often sang with the local opera company.

When Dr. John Barton stood up to preach, Savannah's mind began to wander away, a symptom her mother referred to as "wool gathering." She thought about the children who had lost their parents as a result of the tornado. The memories brought back her own pain at losing her father at such a young age.

> *"Woe to those who make unjust laws, to those who issue oppressive decrees, to deprive the poor of their rights and withhold justice from the oppressed of my people."* Dr. Barton read from the Bible.

Savannah's attention was directed to her Bible as it lay open to Isaiah 10.

"Making widows their prey and robbing the fatherless," he finished the passage and had her undivided attention. Dr. Barton was aware of the hurt felt by many in his congregation and had geared his sermon to bring them comfort. "In Isaiah we see how God comforted His chosen people in the Old Testament times. Today God gives us the Holy Spirit to comfort us through devastating situations."

Savannah's coldness began to melt as she internalized Dr. Barton's message.

"What was true centuries ago is still true today," he said. "God still comforts His people, if they will turn to Him. We must acknowledge God and His presence, so He can provide us with the comfort only He gives, no matter the circumstance."

By the time the invitation was given, Savannah's attitude had changed. "Tom is still alive and therein is the hope for a miracle," she thought.

"Mom, let me take you out for lunch," Savannah said gently nudging her mother's elbow.

"But I have a chicken salad already made at home," her mother protested.

"You can have it for your lunches this week. In fact it'll be even better. I have a strong desire for some fried shrimp from the Mayflower Café."

"Well, that does sound good. Okay" she hesitated. "My car or yours?"

"Let's take the Mustang. It will be easier to park downtown."

Always crowded on Sundays, the Mayflower had a waiting list, but managed to seat Savannah and Mary Ann within 10 minutes. Fried fish and hot grease filled their nostrils causing their empty stomachs to churn and growl as the two ladies began a Sunday ritual of rehashing the sermon. They settled into a booth beneath the fading mural of the Pilgrim's flagship, the *Mayflower*, the restaurant's namesake, while they mused over Dr. Barton's expositional preaching and his remarkable way of using current events to relate to God's unchanging message.

"Only Dr. Barton can correlate the tornado to the tragedies of Isaiah's time," said Mary Ann raising her quiet voice above the clanging of dishes and cacophony of patrons and servers.

"That's what I was thinking," agreed Savannah.

A frumpy, middle-aged woman in a gray uniform with a white apron and box hat interrupted their conversation with, "Good afternoon ladies, what can I get for you today?"

The menu at the Mayflower was only one page because their specialty was often called, "died, fried and laid to the side" seafood or chicken fried steak. No matter what entrée was ordered, it came with a choice of cold slaw or house salad and homemade biscuits or hush puppies. The desserts were always a favorite whether it was the fruit cobbler, in season of course, or pecan pie with ice cream, or a choice of lemon or chocolate meringue pie. Whatever was ordered was homemade on the premises and kept customers returning.

"I'll have the fried shrimp with cold slaw and hush puppies," replied Savannah.

"I'd like the chicken fried steak and a salad with balsamic vinegar dressing, please."

"And what to drink?" the waitress asked.

"Oh, sweet tea for both of us," added Mary Ann.

"God uses so many events in His people's lives to get their attention so they will trust in Him, not in their own abilities," Savannah picked up their discussion of the sermon as if the waitress had not even been there. "You know I just can't help wondering what lesson God is teaching me with Tom's tragedy. It's just so hard for me to understand. When I see him lying on the bed, hooked up to machines, he just isn't the same man I have known for all these years."

"Tragedy is a part of life. It is a part of loving and caring for others. God doesn't promise us that we won't have troubles. What He does promise is that He will be with us in time of trouble, and that we are to remain faithful to Him," Mary Ann spoke softly through her years of wisdom and experience. She understood her daughter's pain only too well. It wasn't just sympathy she had for her youngest, but empathy for a difficult time.

"I know, Mom. I have seen how you have been faithful all these years. It hasn't been easy raising Liz and me. But you did it and God has blessed you for it. You are a pillar of strength to us, yet you are as gentle as a dove. You epitomize the delicacy and fragility of a magnolia blossom, but the strength of the Rock of Gibraltar. I don't know how you do it."

"It is only with the help of Jesus. I pray a lot, for others and myself. Prayer is what changes attitudes and lives."

When their food was served, they stopped briefly to give thanks before resuming the discussion of the sermon.

"When I saw Wanda's name on the list of those killed by the tornado," said Savannah as she purposely stabbed a golden fried shrimp with the tongs of her fork, "my stomach just rolled up like a ball. All I could think about was that we were her family and now we'd lost such a lovely soul. Why her? But I guess you could say, 'why fill in the blank?' Tragedy may be a part of life, but it seems so cruel. I know God is in control, that He is sovereign over all lives and events, but some things are just so hard to swallow."

"We have to remember what Paul wrote in Romans 8:28 that 'all things work together for the good of those who are called according to His purpose.' Savannah, we can't always see the purpose in life—in the bad things as well as the good ones. Sometimes it is years before we can look back and see how God orchestrated events to mold us, shape us and stretch us into His image."

"I know it's not what happens to you in life; it's how you handle it. Like you always say, Mom, we have to have an *attitude of gratitude*. You are so different from Tom's mom. She seems to think she is entitled to only the best things—at least those things that *she* deems best—in life. I saw her

---

sitting in church today, looking like the Queen of England in her regalia, in the balcony so she could look down her nose at everyone. I've tried to be friends with her, but she is so cold. Do you think she really is a Christian?"

"Now, Savannah, you know it is not yours or my place to judge anyone. We don't know what is in her heart. I'm sure she is hurting for Tom since his accident. She had such high expectations for him and now he just lies there as you said, 'hooked up to machines.' It was devastating to me to loose my loving Bryan, but to see your child suffer is an even greater misery. I don't know if I could have stood having something awful happen to one of my girls. No, my heart goes out to her. If she is stoic, it may be because it is her way of coping with such a loss."

"I'm sorry. It was catty of me to say something like that about Barbara. I just hate it that she moved Tom so far away from me. I miss him. I want him close to me. I want him back."

Savannah fought back the tears. She was in public and not the place to break down. As she struggled to maintain her decorum, she realized that it took a certain amount of stoicism to handle herself properly—just like her mother-in-law. Whether she called it stoicism or keeping a "stiff upper lip," it was about maintaining proper behavior for the time and place. Maybe she could look differently at her mother-in-law and see things from her perspective. She silently vowed to try as she focused on devouring the very best fried shrimp anyone could find north of Biloxi.

"Mom, has Mr. Brown been able to do anything more about my being Tom's guardian?" she brightened with a new topic.

"Not really, honey. You know he has this trial right now and pro bono work just takes a backseat. He has filed a petition to name you guardian on the basis that the power of attorney was prior to your marriage, but it will take a month or two for it to appear on the county judge's docket."

"So, does that mean I'm still out of luck with getting him back here?"

"I'm afraid so. But we will keep working on it. I promise."

About 15 miles away, as the crow flies, Barbara and Billy Bob were having their Sunday lunch at their favorite Primos Restaurant on North State Street. Seated in a booth where the windows faced the parking lot that separated the restaurant from the busy street, the Whitehalls finished their New York strip steaks, a main fare on the menu, and were involved in a discussion with Mitch Adams.

"I definitely think you have enough evidence for a law suit," said Mitch. "Here are copies of the photos I have of the pipe that broke when he grabbed it. Look at these ridges," he said pointing to the end of the pipe in the black and white photo.

"How did you get these pictures?" asked Billy Bob.

"Look, don't ask questions you don't want the answer to. I got them. They are real and they spell liability."

"Yes, but who is liable?" the older man retorted. "Do you know who did this or why?"

"No," the investigator ashamedly admitted, "but I'm working on it."

"Well, when you know the answers, come back to see me. But until then, there is not enough here for any lawsuit and if you want to get paid, do the work," Billy Bob growled.

With that Mitch gathered up the photos, placed them neatly in an 11" x 14" manila envelope. "I will be back and I will have the answers," he asserted as he stood to make his way to the front door.

Once he was out of earshot, Barbara asked, "Who would do such a thing?"

"I don't know, but one way or another, JPD is going to pay."

"Do you mean someone on the police force would do such a thing?"

"Well, I don't know who, but it was a training accident and JPD was responsible for the training."

"Do you think one of the people setting up the training did it," she asked placing her napkin on the table.

"Well, I think we need to look at who would benefit from putting him out of commission."

"I see. Guess we'll have to wait for what Mitch finds out."

"That's what I pay him for!"

Monday morning brought a new flood of activity to Savannah's overworked staff. Without Wanda they were at a loss. Savannah needed to hire a replacement, but that would take time and nobody could really replace Wanda. Phone calls kept coming in faster than they could answer them, but she and Doug used the same fact sheet to reply to the many questions fired at them. Her community relations specialist and the newsletter editor pitched in to help field phone calls.

"Stick to the facts and don't go beyond them in speculation," she told them. "We can't give the status of individuals; they have to come from the family. So, essentially, all we can say is if the person is still in our hospital, been discharged, or never been admitted here."

At first blush, it looked like their day was simply confirming the list or not. But as the phone calls rolled in and patients' conditions or status changed, keeping up with so many people became a nightmare for the short-handed staff. It was 3 p.m. before Savannah realized that lunch had long since come and gone. There was no Wanda to call and order lunch for the staff. No Wanda to organize the chaos. No Wanda to field the calls. No Wanda to do the hundreds of things she did effortlessly.

"Okay people, let's put the phones on the night ring for a while and grab a bite from the cafeteria."

"Sounds like a plan to me," Doug responded as he programmed the phones. "Where did the time go?"

"On the way back from our lunch, I'll stop by Webster's office and get the latest list of patients and find a good time for the press conference. We need to give them something for the evening news."

"Don't we have the majority of the casualties or did St. Dominic's get more?"

"Why don't you call over there and find out how many they have listed? Also, call the Baptist Med for their numbers. That will be an important fact to have for the press conference. We should consider meeting the media outside the building so they will have a better background for their reports. The emergency room area is off limits, but what do you think about the main door facing Woodrow Wilson?"

"Hey, that's great with the afternoon sun shining on it. It should be perfect. Shall I start calling when I get back to the office?"

"Yeah, the four local networks for TV, the *Clarion-Ledger*, the two wire services, and WSLI radio. That should do it. We'll just plan on it for 4:30, so they'll have time to get back to the station or do a live shot at six."

For the next two weeks UMMC's PR team handled a multitude of follow up requests about the tornado victims and their perpetually fluctuating status. Each day seemed to stretch longer than the one before. Without a break, except for Sunday mornings, Savannah was exhausted. Finally, she allowed herself a Saturday off and planned to stay in bed until 10 o'clock. However, shortly after seven, the phone jarred her awake.

"Savannah, aren't you going to Atlanta to see Tom with us today?" inquired the terse voice of her mother-in-law.

"Uh, well, it's been a really rough week and I had not planned to," she began without really thinking about what she had been asked.

Nonetheless, she was cut off in mid-sentence by, "I see where your priorities are. Well, just remember, we offered you an opportunity to fly down with us. This will not bode well for you."

The phone was dead before she even had time to process the conversation. And what did Barbara mean about it would not "bode well?" She lay beneath the covers trying to sort things out in her mind. Barbara was up to something, but what?

Her body ached from all the tension. She wanted to sleep, but her mind wouldn't let her. Flashes of Wanda's funeral on Thursday kept eating at her. Few people attended the services at Baldwin Funeral Home and only a handful of friends accompanied Wanda's casket to the gravesite on

Robinson Road. Death and destruction had hit Savannah personally again. Life was fragile and she wanted to make the right choices. Doing what was just and right was not the easy path to take.

She questioned her decision to not go with the Whitehalls to Atlanta, but Barbara really didn't ask her to go until this morning. That was what really bothered her. How could she have planned to go, if she didn't know she was invited to fly with them? Certainly she would have jumped at the chance to be with Tom. Sleep was something she could always do later. There was more to this than her not being asked until the last minute to go. The entire incident left her in a malaise.

At Billy Bob and Barbara's house a loud discussion erupted from the master bedroom. Although Pearl stood at the kitchen sink, the shrill voices caused her to shake her head and mutter, "That poor child, that poor child."

"Why in heaven's name did you call her if you didn't want her to go?" Billy Bob asked.

"We have to establish a pattern on her part of not caring and not being supportive. Don't you know anything?"

"I know who makes the money and who spends the money around here!"

"Well, I'm trying to protect your money and keep that hussy from getting her sticky paws on it."

"What makes you so certain that it's my money she's after anyway? Tom has already thumbed his nose at my money with his job and showed no interest in his inheritance."

"And who bought that cute little townhouse she's living in now?"

"We did, but that was in lieu of the honeymoon to the Bahamas."

"But Tom isn't enjoying it now, is he? No, he's off in Atlanta and she isn't even going to visit him. She should quit that job. It takes all the time she should spend with him."

"Then she would be after my money to pay her bills!"

"Billy Bob, you are impossible to talk to. Is the plane ready for us?"

"It will be by the time we get to the airport. Why don't you just lay off for a while? You stir up more hornets' nests than I can shake a stick at. Speaking of hornets' nests, what has the PI found out?"

"I told him to find out when little miss Prissy arrived at the competition site. He's working on that and finding out how or who sabotaged that bar. He's supposed to get back to me by Monday."

"Well, he better get some answers. I'm paying him enough. And so far the only info he has given me is that the bar had marks of being sawed. I doubt if Savannah had anything to do with that."

Chapter 10

S taring out at the white billows dotting the blue horizon, Savannah's thoughts retreated to last month's debacle with her mother-in-law. She was flying to Atlanta for Tom's birthday, but the bitterness of Barbara's abrupt phone call clouded the joy she should be experiencing. How did Barbara steal her joy? It had been an impossible situation for Savannah—a last minute invitation—and she didn't even have time to react. What was she to do? She had missed an opportunity to see Tom and that hurt the most. After an early morning run with the Harriers and to avoid an afternoon of loneliness, she spent the rest of Saturday at the office finishing projects. Saturdays were supposed to be spent with Tom, lingering over an extra cup of coffee, studying his grey eyes, cuddling in bed, or doing their "road work" together. Running wasn't the same with the Harriers and doing housework was mundane. She had taken such pride in maintaining a spotless home, but without Tom the motivation dwindled.

Her eyes strayed to the window again. The cumulus clouds conjured up images reminiscent of her childhood when each puff appeared as a different object or animal. Running and playing on a carpet of freshly cut Saint Augustine blades with the sweet scent of roses and lilacs had been such happy times, but seemed like eons ago. Before she had completed the thought, the pilot interrupted with his announcement of their final approach to Atlanta's Hartsfield airport. The local temperature was 95 degrees with clear skies, about normal for the third week of June.

"Yes," Savannah thought, "I'll see Tom and get to hold his hand in mine. If only the circumstances . . ." But she could not dwell on that. It was time to put on her game face "to make mama proud." Shoring up for the game was the right thing to do, but it wasn't easy and nobody ever promised her that. All she had to do was look at her mom and see that sometimes it was struggling through the difficult times that made you into the best person you could be. Joseph, Israel's son had always been an example Mary Ann used to encourage her daughters. What Joseph's brothers had planned for evil, the Lord had used for good and saved the nation of Israel.

"No, I'm not going to save anyone's life," Savannah thought. "I see doctors doing that every day, so what can I do? I just keep on keeping on and hope that God will use me in some way. I am grateful for having Tom, even if it has only been three years."

She said a silent prayer of thanks as the wheels bounced down the tarmac. Yes, this was her life for now.

One hospital was like any other hospital, except for their areas of specialties, which was based on the expertise of the doctors who practiced there. Atlanta's rehab facility provided private suites as well as semi-private rooms. Tom's room was private because Billy Bob and Barbara insisted on it. But this was nice for Savannah, too. She could talk to Tom without worrying about prying ears straining to hear her and a secure place to grab a nap.

All was well as she curled up in the recliner at the foot of his bed—that is until.

"Well, Billy Bob, lookie who's here! I thought you weren't coming, missy. That you had too much work to do!" taunted Barbara as she made her grand entrance.

"Hello, Savannah," Billy Bob demurred, trying hastily to harness his haughty wife. He was normally flamboyant in his own way, but when Barbara got her back up, there was no comparison.

"Hi, how was your flight?" Savannah queried to deflect her mother-in-law's barbs as she stood up. "Would you like to sit here?"

"Oh, heaven's no," Barbara retorted. "We won't be here long. I just wanted to check on my baby boy and make sure he is being well-cared for. Besides, we'll be back when you leave for the evening."

"Well, actually, I have made arrangements for the nurse to bring me a blanket and pillow, so I can just sleep here."

"You can't sleep here!" she bellowed at her daughter-in-law.

"Sure she can," interjected Billy Bob.

"Whose side are you on?" she screamed. "You can't be defending this little gold digger!"

"Aw honey, I'm just saying that the hospital allows it. Why don't we go talk to the head nurse and get the report we came for. You can see there is no apparent change in Tommy."

Billy Bob gently put his arm around his wife's shoulder turning her toward the door. After nearly 35 years of marriage, he knew mellowness was the only way to calm his supercilious love. He knew the secret of a long marriage was "always do everything your wife wants and make more money than she can spend." Billy Bob was good at doing both. Moving his wife to another location was the only way to diffuse this situation.

"Honey, we have a beautiful suite waiting for us. We can order room service or go out for dinner. Whatever you want," he cooed not even giving her time to respond, just moving her down the hallway.

Savannah trembled as she moved closer to Tom's bedside. "Oh, Tom, I miss you so much. I know I need to be strong, but I'd sure like to be able to lean on you for a while. This isn't the life we planned. I guess Miriam was right about playing the hand you're dealt. It sure seems unfair to see you lying there, just wasting away before my eyes. The once strong, handsome man, who was hardly ever still now unmoving, eyes closed to the world you couldn't wait to see. But I will always be here for you. I'll be waiting for you when you do wake up. I know you will one day. I love you," she concluded kissing his forehead.

There were no pictures of smiling faces, double fudge cake with 25 candles, or beautifully wrapped presents for Tom this year. He wouldn't remember this June 25th, but Savannah would never forget the chocolate cupcake Georgia Kane purchased for her from the Atlanta Bakery Shoppe and delivered to Tom's room. She had looked all over Jackson for the perfect card, but did not find it until she stopped by the hospital gift shop. Its simple words spoke volumes for Savannah's heart. It said:

Happy Birthday to the man of my dreams,
To the reason for the sun shining,
To the one for whom my heart sings,
And for whom I'm always pining.

That was her Tom. She read the card to him and placed it on the window sill. Both her heart and her head ached. Encounters with Barbara were always strenuous to her, but unavoidable. She never knew what her mother-in-law would do next.

Even though she had grown up knowing the Whitehalls, she had managed to avoid Barbara's warpath until college. When she and Tom had dated in high school, Barbara was courteous to her, but always stand-offish and kept her distance. It was actually easier than these confrontations, especially without Tom to run interference.

Settling into the hospital recliner, she pulled out her Bible and read to him from her favorite Psalm passages. It lifted her spirits as well as soothed her emotions. Then she turned to Paul's writings that spoke of hope for the Philippines. She concluded her readings with Paul's love letter in First Corinthians, chapter 13. Dr. Barton had read this at their wedding and each anniversary they read it together.

Laying her Bible down, she went to his bedside and began tenderly stroking his forehead. Softly she sang love songs, including their favorite, "Cherished." Although his breathing was mechanical and his eyelids closed, she connected his heart with hers. She could imagine that somewhere inside he sang the songs with her to commemorate his birthday and their third anniversary.

"Happiness is a temporary state of being depending on the circumstances," she told him, "but joy comes from deep within your soul. I am happy to be with you, but not happy with the circumstances. But my joy resonates from within me because of the love you and I share. God is the third partner of our marriage and His love gives both of us a joy to share. I know you can hear me within your soul and I know that we are still connected in our spirits. Our lives are not what we had envisioned them to be, but God is still with us and joining us together as one. It is with God that we will be joined forever, no matter what happens in this temporal life. I will love you forever, Tom."

For the next two days Savannah did not leave Tom's room except for a few quick trips to the hospital's canteen. Food was not her concern, the man hooked up to tubes and contraptions suspended from the ceiling that periodically raised and lowered his limbs, was the focus of her attention. She read aloud from her Bible and from the books on her Kindle, which she had downloaded prior to coming. She enjoyed biographies and autobiographies about ordinary people who accomplished extraordinary things in their lives like John Maxwell, Corrie ten Boom, and Elisabeth Elliot. But she also read some of Tom's favorites like the *Lord of the Rings* trilogy.

Reading turned the hours into minutes—but never enough time. Time crept along and then it was gone. Her time was up and she was forced to leave Tom once again.

Her reservations were on the last flight back to Jackson on Sunday night. She gathered her personal belongings and stuffed them into the carry-on bag, kissed Tom and said good-bye. Her cab waited outside the main entrance.

"Where to, ma'am?" asked the olive-skinned man with a thick Asian accent.

"The airport," she replied almost under her breath. It was an expensive trip, but sometimes money is well-spent no matter the cost. Savannah had always been thrifty, but spending time with Tom was priceless.

Chapter 11

Work was therapeutic for the PR professional and UMMC was always humming with newsworthy research projects. Richard Roddenburg's breakthrough treatment of paralysis was of particular interest to Savannah. Even though his parents transferred Tom to Atlanta, Roddenburg continued to monitor Tom's progress through Bradley Cummings, a former classmate at Vanderbilt and head of neurology in Atlanta's rehab facility. Spinal injuries were their specialty and Tom's prolonged coma piqued their interest.

"Hi, doc," Savannah called seeing Roddenburg in the foyer of the neurology suite. "I just spent the weekend with Tom."

"Really?" he queried. "Any change?"

"Well, he's still in the coma, but, you know I could almost feel like he knew I was there."

"The brain is a marvelous organ. I'll ask Brad to recheck the print outs monitoring his neurological activity. I wish we could have kept him here."

"Me, too. But I had nothing to do with it."

"Why would your in-laws want to inconvenience you and them by moving him so far away? We have a great, nearly new rehab center here."

"You've got me, doc. But I'm sure my mother-in-law was at the center of that decision, and knowing her, there is an ulterior motive. Let me know if you have anything significant. I did hear that your car accident patient is walking on-his-own. Are you ready to talk to the media about him?"

"Soon, very soon. I have a few more tests to perform before we do that."

"Okay, I'll check with you later. This is definitely one of your best success stories and we want to let the world know. Will you be writing it up for one of the medical journals?"

"I will, but I want to make sure everything is just right and that we don't make any false assumptions or statements. You know we have to have proof, not just hypotheses."

"Good point. Well, when you are ready, let me know."

"I definitely will."

"Mrs. Whitehall, Tom's charts indicate an improvement in his brain activity," Dr. Cummings, announced to Barbara when he saw her exiting one of the rooms at the rehab center.

"Really?" she questioned after spending an hour reading one of her romance novels in the chair next to Tom's bed.

"I knew bringing my son here would be the best thing for him. And what do you attribute this change to?"

"Well, it all corresponds to his wife's visit this weekend. Let me show you the chart."

"I am not interested in seeing what her visit did or did not do. And as far as I'm concerned, you can just throw that chart away," she huffed before spinning on her heels and heading to the hospital's front door where Billy Bob dutifully waited.

Barbara was punctual and expected everyone else to be on time. It was an admirable trait that was not lost on Billy Bob, because time was money to him. They had spent enough time with their son and were ready to fly back to Jackson, where business meetings waited for Billy Bob and the country club ladies would meet his wife. The ladies were planning their summer charity events that were more self-ingratiating than they were accommodating to their recipients.

Barbara's friends, most of whom were in her Sunday school class or her bridge group at the country club had moved up from the Junior League of Jackson and the society pages of the *Clarion-Ledger* to be leaders of various charities. Charity balls solicited money for the arts, not for the poor, homeless, or downtrodden. A token amount would be given to benevolence funds, but their focus was improving the operas, the Little Theater's performances, and supporting the Jackson Symphony Orchestra. They were reasonable causes for improving Jackson's cultural arts and ensuring top quality talents and performances, but it was mostly for their entertainment.

At the end of June the bright sun lit the entire reserved parking lot as Savannah made her way to the car. She saw no one, nor anything suspicious, but there was a tingling up her spine indicating she was being watched. But who would be watching her? And why? Her life was an open book to those around her. Yet, there it was. That sense of being like an animal at the zoo with someone curiously observing her every move.

Mitch flicked another cigarette out the window and thinking about this job. He was after someone who wanted to maim or kill a policeman. But his boss wanted him to follow the wife, too. He really couldn't figure out why he was following her. If it was a divorce case like the ones he normally handled, then there would be romantic interludes with people sneaking around to motels and creating some really juicy pictures. But with this dame, he could set his watch by what she did. Work, home, church and shopping. The only real interesting part of her day was her occasional run with some group. But that seemed to be limited to Saturdays. He could take photos all day and there would be nothing—unless she was seeing someone at work. She worked long hours—maybe that was it. Maybe he could find some dirt there.

He cranked his Charger and pulled out of the space in the parking garage. It had been the perfect spot to observe those departing from the north side of UMMC. He could follow Savannah without detection because he already knew the route she took unless she stopped for groceries at the Jitney Jungle. Then she'd take Lakeland Drive instead of going north to County Line Road.

"Which way are we going, missy?" he pondered.

"*To know, know, know you is love, love, love you,*" sang Savannah along with the radio as she pulled into her garage. Her radio was always set to easy-listening music, never hard rock. It calmed her and allowed her to decompress from her day, especially when the traffic was crazy. Stepping out of the car she inhaled the aromatic crape myrtles in full bloom. From behind the townhouse she heard the lake lapping against the boulders surrounding the reservoir. Surveying her garden she eyed the azalea bushes that had long lost their blossoms, but noted the white gardenias gracing the front door with their tantalizing perfume, coveted by cosmetic companies. A smile incased her face as she spotted the geraniums peeking out between the azaleas. She remembered that Pat, Tom's former partner, brought the bright red geranium to his room the day of the accident, as she inspected her garden. There were a few sprigs of grass that needed plucking, she noted unmindful that someone scrutinized her every move.

Mitch cruised slowly down the street. "Thanks for keeping to your schedule," he smirked. He had other places to go and people to see that were more exciting to him.

That partially sawed pole held his interest more than Savannah. Mr. Whitehall was paying him to get to the truth about his son's accident. Mrs. Whitehall wanted to find dirt on her daughter-in-law. For Mitch the easier task was finding out why the metal bar on one of the confidence course stations had saw marks. It was the last location or task to complete the course and would have been a true test for anyone. But the final event had held an additional challenge. And the metal bar lying on his front passenger seat certainly intrigued him as to why it was not intact. Why? That was the real question.

The next day his first stop was a small shop on Gallatin Street in South Jackson. A former high school buddy owned Mister Fixit and Jimmy had innate abilities when it came to mechanical engineering.

"Hey, Jimbo, how's it going," he called entering the sweltering open bay of Mister Fixit. It was basically a tin-roofed barn with a few ceiling fans to stir the air and a couple of oscillating fans directed at work benches. Metal shelves lined the walls under large case windows with grease and grime laden tables stationed in the middle of the floor. Grinders, a drill press, and a myriad of table saws dotted the work benches that had seen better days.

"Well, Mitch, long time no see. What's up?"

"Yeah, well, you know how time gets away from you. I got this puzzling case I'm working on and could use a little help."

"You still spying on people?"

"I guess you could call it that, but it pays the bills. And with all the divorces nowadays, I get plenty of business. But this is a little different. I've got this metal rod here and am trying to figure out what happened to it."

"Let me see. Umm. Looks like it's been sawed on both ends. What's it go to?"

"You know that police training site out in Rankin County?"

"Yeah, I've heard about it."

"This was part of a confidence station and broke off during a big competition."

"That didn't break off, my friend. It was sawed off!"

"Well, there was a competitor who grabbed this bar and was supposed to swing down to the next bar, but the bar broke and sent him down with it."

"It was no accident. Look at these teeth marks on both ends. Someone did this deliberately. There would be no reason for these teeth marks unless someone planned for it to fail."

"That's what I was thinking, but I wanted someone who knows how these things are put together to tell me. I just can't figure out why someone would saw it before the competition. How would they know when it would break?"

"You can figure how much stress will be needed to break the bar. From that determine how many foot-pounds would be required to finish the job."

"You can do that?"

"Sure. It's simple, mass times pressure. You know like lumberjacks figuring how to make a tree fall the direction and at time they are ready. But to make it fall the direction you want, you have chip away part of one side, then saw through from the opposite direction you want it to fall. So, with this bar, you calculate the tinsel strength of the bar, then pounds or pressure to break that. By sawing at both ends, you can diminish the strength by a coefficient of the rate of tinsel strength."

"But how would you know when it would break?"

"You take the average weight of the competitors and divide that into the tinsel strength. That will tell you approximately how many repetitions on it will be needed to bring it down."

"You make it sound so simple."

"It is. It's just a mathematical equation."

"So, the person who planned this would have to know all this about tinsel strength and the right mathematical equation?"

"Yeah, but it doesn't take a genius to figure it out."

"So, it could be anybody."

"Well, let's say, if you wanted to make sure it was a certain person, then you would have to know things, like the line-up of competitors, their weights, or approximately, and other conditions on the course. Like does everyone do this station first or is it last on the list. It could be affected by how hard they grip the bar, if they swing on it, or if they use one or two hands."

"I guess that narrows down the field of people who could have done it."

"Yes, and you may need to consider when it was done. How long before the competition they sawed it. Was it inspected before the competition or not?"

"Hey, you've given me a lot to think about. Looks like I've got more investigating to do. Thanks for your help."

"Any time and don't be such a stranger."

"Okay, Jimmy. You take care of yourself. Looks like things are going well for you here," Mitch noted the shelves lined with small engine parts and the work tables cluttered with half-finished projects.

"I do okay. But I really like being my own boss and doing what I enjoy."

"Can't get better than that, can it? See ya."

"See you around."

"Hey, Ron, how's life treating you?" Mitch asked as he barged into the office of the chief of police.

Two weeks had passed since his encounter with his classmate and now he was calling in another chip. But that's the way a good PI worked. It wasn't just what you know, but knowing who to ask when you didn't know. His days on the force had been good until his wife left him. His drinking had been the problem, but he wasn't sure if it started before she left, caused her to leave, or just got worse when she left. But a DUI was not tolerated by the previous chief and a 12-year veteran lost it all in one night. There was no forgiveness, no second chance, even when he joined AA. Knowing his propensity to not stop after one drink, he swore off anything with more kick than a caffeinated soda.

"Well, look what the cat drug in that the dog wouldn't have. If it ain't Mitchell Adams as I live and breathe. You old son of a gun, how you been?"

"Doing well, doing well."

"Knowing you, this isn't a social visit."

"You know me well, don't you, Ron? Guess that comes from all those days we pounded the streets together as rookies. And of course those stakeouts we spent together. Not too many secrets we didn't share, were there?"

"Nope. We solved a lot of the world's problems. Too bad we couldn't solve our own. You still married to that sweet little blondie?"

"Negative, she left me before I left the force. Guess she didn't think we had much of a future with no kids and all work. It's okay though 'cause the hours I work these days I'm home even less."

"Same ole Mitch, still making excuses. Well, what can I do for you?"

"I'm doing some PI work for a client who is interested in one of your special unit members. He was recently injured during a training camp. Could I get a list of everyone participating in the competition at the Rankin County facility March 28?"

"You know there was something strange about that accident that we just couldn't figure. So, what do you know about it?"

"Not much really, but it may not have been an accident. However, we need to keep this close hold because if there was foul play, then it may be someone involved with the competition."

"You don't say? Tell you what, I'll give you access to whatever you need, but you only ask me for the info. And this stays just between you and me, got it?"

"Absolutely! Not a problem with me. At this point I just have a bunch of hunches."

Chief Bennett made an about face to open the large wooden file cabinet behind his massive oak desk. The office was nicely furnished with a leather couch under his "I love me" wall which included a menagerie of trophies, plaques and certificates, as well as his college diploma from Southern. The windows on the left wall gave a bird's eye view of downtown, straight to the Capitol Building. There were perks for being police chief at the state's capitol.

Pulling a folder from one of the lateral file drawers, Ron said, "Here you go, a complete list of participants from Mississippi, Louisiana and Alabama. Just one question, do you think it was one of ours or theirs?"

"Sorry, Ron, I don't have a clue yet. Does this tell when the teams arrived?"

"Not here, but we may have a list with the reservations we took. Let me look."

Ron rummaged through his desk drawer and came up with another folder.

"Here it is. My secretary took all the reservations, so this will show approximate arrival times for the teams."

"Thanks. This will help a lot."

"Now listen, Mitch, you take good care of that info. If I didn't trust you so much, I wouldn't let it out of my sight."

"I know, I know. I'll return it the way I got it."

"And, Mitch, one more thing, I want to get to the bottom of this. Tom is one of my best special ops guys and to boot, his old man is a big shot, not just in Jackson, but in the state. He carries a mighty big stick."

"Yes, I know he does. Believe me; I am all too well aware of it."

"Say, his old man isn't your client, is it?"

"Now, Ron, you know I can't tell you that. Besides it is better if you don't know. But when I have pertinent information, I will definitely share it with you."

The former partners shook hands before the PI lumbered out the door. He had put on weight since his days at JPD because he lacked the self-discipline to work-out and over indulged in fast-food. In the elevator he began scanning the two file folders.

"Names," he muttered. "Just a bunch of names. What do they mean?"

Chapter 12

“**M**om, I don't know how I'm going to get time off to visit Tom this month," Savannah lamented as she stared out the windows of her office. "At least last month I had the fourth to give me an extra day for the trip to Atlanta. But there aren't any holidays this month and I don't have any vacation time left."

"Can you take a sick day?"

"I used all the days I had accrued when Tom first went there."

"Haven't you accrued any since then?"

"I think it has been only a few hours, but I will certainly call HR about it. There are some special circumstances, but normally they are for pregnancy or have to do with childcare. If I was sick, then I could ask for others to donate sick days, but with it being Tom, it changes all the rules."

"If you combine a sick day with a weekend, then it would make your travel that much easier."

"You're right. But these airline tickets aren't cheap."

"I can help you out with that, honey."

"Oh, Mom, I don't need that. I guess I'm just whiney today and needed to let it out. I just get so frustrated thinking about how he could be right here and I could see him every day. But, no, I have to limit my visits with him because he's in Atlanta, thanks to Barbara."

"I understand. Have you heard from her or Billy Bob lately?"

"No, I haven't and I'm not sure what to make of it. The last time I spoke to her was in June when we were both at the Atlanta hospital. That was such an awkward, awful time. It would just be so much easier if he were here."

Millie Engels, Savannah's recently hired administrative assistant, rapped on the doorframe.

"Excuse me, Mrs. Whitehall, but you have a call on line two from a Mitch Adams. I can take a message, if you want. But he said it was urgent."

"No, Millie, I'll be with him in a second," she replied swinging back around to face her desk. "Mom, I need to take this call. I'll call you when I get home."

"Okay, you be careful driving home."

"Thanks for listening to me whine, Mom. Love you."

Millie disappeared to her desk and Savannah pushed the button on line two.

"Savannah Whitehall, how may I help you?"

"Mrs. Whitehall, my name is Mitch Adams and I'm a private investigator looking in to your husband's accident. I need your help."

"Why are you looking at Tom's accident and why in the world would you need my help?"

"Well, it's complicated. You see, I have reason to believe that it wasn't really an accident, that it was sabotage," Mitch explained. He had followed her to work on several occasions and discovered that work was all she did at UMMC. Even talking to some of the staff had revealed nothing out of the ordinary, so he felt sure she would help him.

"What do you mean, sabotage? Who? Why would someone do such a thing?"

"Well, to be honest with you, that's what I'm hoping you can help me with."

"I can't imagine how I can help, but by all means, I'd like to try. What do you need from me?"

"Information. Sensitive information. You probably know all the guys in the competition and I know I can trust what you tell me. So, will you help me investigate some of these guys from the competition?"

Mitch knew how to work his informants, no matter who they were. Now that she was no longer his suspect, he could be straight with her and not resort to his manipulative powers that normally increased his successes.

"Well, I do know the guys Tom worked with, but not the teams from out of state."

"It's Tom's teammates I need your help with."

"Okay, but what can I do?"

"Well, I have a list of names to read to you and you just tell me anything you can remember about them—especially if Tom has talked about them or worked special cases with them. Anything significant about them you can relate to."

Mitch began reading the list of names of those attending the competition. When it came to members of Jackson's team, Savannah only had positive comments about them. Tom had always spoken highly of his squad—no one she knew had an ounce of deviousness, as far as she could tell. No, Tom never mentioned anything but a great relationship with all the guys. What about someone who was not on his team?

Did anyone show up that wasn't a part of the competition? Did they all visit Tom at the hospital? Was there anything suspicious about their visits?

"I don't remember seeing anyone who wasn't supposed to be there. I can't imagine someone being there if they weren't supposed to be."

"Really? Well, according to the list there were support people around and they weren't team members. I got this list from a reliable source."

"Let me think. I did arrive later than anticipated. They had already completed the marksmanship comp, so someone could have been there and gone. Or maybe they were at the other stations. I was at the end of the physical endurance course to see Tom finish. I knew he would be first or at least one of the first."

"So you didn't see anyone at the station when Tom was injured?"

"No, I'm not sure of that. The EMS guys were there, but when Tom fell things happened so fast and they jumped into action. Besides, I couldn't swear to anything after that because my focus was completely on Tom."

"Yes, I'm sure it was. But what about who came to see Tom later, can you tell me about who visited him?"

"Well, the first guys were from IA. But then Chris O'Donnell went to high school with Tom and played football together. They both joined the police force the same year but went through the police academy at different times. I think Tom was accepted first because his degree is in criminal justice. But they were friends, as far as I could tell. Maybe a little competitive jealousy. I think that may be why Chris moved from SWAT to Internal Affairs. Tom was so good at his job that not many could keep up with him. But that's the way it was with Tom. The other guys on the team looked to him as their leader naturally."

"Ummm, I see. Well, this is good info. It gives me something to start with."

"You can't think it was any of the guys at the competition, can you? They are all such a close knit group. Even Chris used to run with us on the week-ends. We ran with a group called the Hash House Harriers once or twice a month. And he's the first one who came to visit Tom at the hospital."

"You would be surprised what competitive jealousy can do for over-achievers. I used to be a policeman, so I know what it's like. Is there anyone else on the team that expressed a very competitive spirit, especially to Tom?"

"Gee, those guys were always competitive. Like you said, it's part of their DNA. They all want to be number one and the best at their job. Many times they would be called out for riots and it was a game to see who could collar the most rioters. Tom's former beat partner, Pat O'Brien, was one who would give him a hard time, but it was friendly rivalry. There was a time or two when Mark had to reprimand Pat for getting carried away with his beleaguering attitude."

"Really? And Pat's name is on this list, too. Mark would be Mark Spencer their supervisor, I assume."

"Yes. But Pat and Tom were at the academy together. They've been close a long time. He came to see Tom, too. He just didn't get there until . . ."

"I know, but in my business you suspect everyone until you find hard evidence that they're above suspicion."

"Wow. I just never would have thought that any of these guys would have had anything to do with Tom's accident."

"It's possible. But don't discuss this with anyone, okay?"

115

"Believe me, I won't. It is too incredulous."

"I'm still working on facts. Right now it is all supposition and that's why you cannot talk to anyone about it. Got it?"

"Got it."

"Thanks, Mrs. Whitehall. I may be calling you again, if that's okay?"

"Sure, anything I can do to help."

"And here's my cell number if you think of something."

Mitch gave her his number and they said good-bye with Savannah shaking her head in disbelief. It had not occurred to her that someone purposely injured Tom. She thought everyone loved him. He was always affable and gregarious.

Late August heat and humidity swelled up on the Gulf Coast threatening Mississippi from Biloxi to Jackson with thunderstorms, hurricanes, and tornados. The weather was unpredictable and could change on a moment's notice as the temperature of the Gulf rose. But the summer heat, as violent as it could be, paled in comparison to the heat Barbara turned up on her daughter-in-law. Cunningly Barbara concocted a plan she presented to Dudley Randall, Billy Bob's attorney on retainer.

"Look, Dudley, here's the deal. Savannah and Tom have not lived together since March, that's almost six months. That's the time required for abandonment in a divorce case. And since Tom cannot speak for himself, as the holder of this power of attorney, I want to file for divorce against Savannah Whitehall. They have no children, so this should not be complicated."

"But these are highly unusual circumstances, Mrs. Whitehall," Randall protested. "I don't believe there's a precedent set for this type of divorce proceedings."

"Oh, yes, there is. My mother was awarded her divorce because my father abandoned us."

"I know abandonment is cause for divorce, Mrs. Whitehall, but it is normally when the remaining spouse files because the other one has indicated no intention of returning, as in your mother's case. But even at that, it requires a year of separation. Another case would be living apart, but again that must be for a minimum of three years." "But what about this power of attorney? Could that allow us to speed things up?"

"Perhaps so, but I will need to research it. Nonetheless, we do need to wait until September to petition the court."

"Fine, fine. Whatever it takes. Just get on with it. As soon as possible I want her out of the house we bought and her to have no claims on my son whatsoever. You understand?" she demanded pacing the floor like a caged cockatoo in her powder-blue A-line skirt with matching camel's hair jacket. Twirling her turquoise and sterling silver necklace that cascaded over the silk ruffles of her barely blue blouse, Barbara's demeanor did not portray the prim and proper aristocrat she normally exemplified.

Dudley noted this new persona as he explained the legal issues she faced in such a case. "We could be opening Pandora's Box with this, you realize?"

"That's what we pay you to do. Figure it out so that it is all legal and tied up in a nice bow. I don't want any of it to be challenged; I just want it to work. Okay?"

Shuffling papers on his desk, Dudley rose to walk her out of his office. "I'll take care of it. You just go have a nice lunch with Mr. Whitehall and I'll complete the paperwork," he remarked, trying to placate the highly excitable fox that could turn into a ferocious mama bear without notice.

"You do that," she insisted on having the last word as she closed the mahogany and glass door a little too hard, making it rattle even though it was rather sturdy.

Dudley retreated to the bookcase behind his desk. He would have to research abandonment divorce cases. Abandonment was a legitimate cause for divorce, but this had some quirks even Dudley had never dealt with. And he certainly didn't want to get laughed out of a courtroom for "frivolous filing actions." Most abandonment cases were requested after a year of separation, but that was by a spouse, not a parent. It would create a stir and depending on who was sitting on the bench, it could be extremely dicey.

Dr. Roddenburg's press release on his breakthrough with his paralysis patient should have written itself, but Savannah couldn't concentrate. The technical process of retraining the brain functions were a jungle of foreign words resulting in a fragmented concept of science, in other words, nonsense to her. Finishing the initial release and writing her publicity plan was not going to happen today. She closed the folder, slid it into her desk drawer, and turned out the lights before locking the door.

Merging into rush-hour traffic, Savannah hardly noticed the stop-and-go reaction of the drivers around her. She didn't even turn on the radio as her mind drifted to the Saturday morning at the end of March. She could see it all happening again right before her eyes—Tom lying on the ground, lifeless. At first she thought he was dead, and then was relieved to find he was alive. Then fear and panic struck her as the paramedics loaded him into the ambulance.

Before she realized it, Savannah pulled into the driveway of her and Tom's dream home. For the last five months every time she entered her beautiful home on the Reservoir, emptiness engulfed her entire existence. Without Tom it was just a cute little house, not a home. Her life had changed with this new deck of cards. She played this new game like a robot, responding to demands for her job, for her time, but without passion. The fire and enthusiasm, with which she normally played, had burned out. She still loved her work, but constantly fought the distraction of worrying about Tom. Bottom line, she wanted Tom home where he belonged—with her.

Chapter 13

"It is September the fifteenth, Dudley. Where are the divorce papers?" demanded Barbara as she stormed by the lawyer's secretary.

"I'm sorry, Mr. Randall, but she didn't even give me a chance to announce her arrival," protested Anna Boone, a small woman about 40 who normally commanded the office traffic like a drill sergeant.

"It's all right, Anna. I understand. Don't worry about it," Dudley consoled her. Standing up to greet Barbara he asked, "And how may I help you today, Mrs. Whitehall?"

"You can do what my husband pays you to do."

"I am. I have all the papers ready for your and Mr. Whitehall's signatures."

"Well, why haven't you called us in to sign them?"

"Because, my dear lady, we have to wait until after Sept. 28."

"Whatever for?"

"It must be a minimum of six months before we can even begin to petition the courts to make you guardians of Tom and a year of separation or willful desertion for a divorce."

"We can sign them and you can put whatever date you want to on them."

"It doesn't work like that. They must be notarized for the court to accept them."

"This is just a bunch of nitpicking and you are trying my patience."

"Perhaps so, but we are testing new waters with these divorce proceedings and I want to make sure all my 'i's are dotted and my 't's are crossed before I get laughed out of the judge's chambers. When you are dealing with legal matters, especially if they are provocative—and this one takes the cake—you have to be super meticulous."

"I think you are stalling and I'm not sure why. We pay you enough to do whatever we need."

"But you do not pay me enough to be disbarred, ma'am. This is my profession and I prefer to be scrupulous in how I conduct business. I am happy to help you with any and all legal matters, but I reserve the right to ensure it is always completed within the limits of the laws of this state."

"Well, I'll be back on September 29 with Billy Bob, and you better have those papers ready for me to sign."

"I will, Mrs. Whitehall, as long as everything goes according to the plan."

"You better," she responded leaving in a huff.

"Glad to see that storm blow over," commented Anna when the door slammed.

"Me, too, but it'll be back. You can count on it. I don't mind working for Billy Bob. He has his quirks, but her, that's a totally different story. She's enough to make you lose your religion."

"Amen, Mr. Randall."

With June to November as the primary hurricane season for the Gulf Coast, which usually dumped rain and tornados on central Mississippi, Savannah kept her crisis communication plan readily available. Periodically, she reviewed it, but today she wanted to make sure Millie was thoroughly familiar with it. Wanda's untimely death at North Cross Mall affected her boss' perceptions. It wasn't that Wanda didn't know what to do, she had been extremely capable, but she never stood a chance against an F2 tornado, which has winds from 113 to 157 mph. In 1966 a tornado struck Candlestick Shopping Mall and killed nine people, but that was before Savannah's time. Responding to the destruction and experiencing a personal loss provoked a challenging perspective of the tornados' devastation.

With her mind on the Fujita rating on tornados, Savannah was oblivious to the one that struck the law offices of Milburn, Blackmon and Randall or the storm brewing on the second floor at UMMC. She caught her first indication of wild winds whipping up when her phone rang.

"This is Andrew. There's been a shooting in urology. We need you stat."

Without an audible response, she hung up the phone and ran for the elevator, yelling back at Doug, "Grab your notebook and come with me."

In the elevator, Savannah repeated Andrew's cryptic call. Exiting on the second floor, the duo observed a swarm of activity at the chief of urology's office. One of the hospital guards approached Savannah.

"It looks like a homicide and suicide. This guy just walked in and blew Dr. Sarong away, as far as we can tell.

Then he must have shot himself. What else do you need to know?" the guard asked.

"Do you have his name or how he knew Dr. Sarong?"

"We're working on it, ma'am."

Huddled in a corner chair of the outer office was Sharon Sarong's secretary, trying to make herself invisible. Arms folded around her body and head tucked against her chest, Penny ignored the buzz around her.

"Penny, are you okay?" Savannah asked as she bent down to face the frightened figure.

Raising her head with glazed over eyes; Penny just nodded before resting her chin back on her thorax.

"Do you know this guy, Penny?"

Without looking up, she mumbled, "Uh huh."

"What's his name?"

"Matthew."

"Do you know his last name?" prompted Savannah, realizing that Penny was in shock and required extra coaxing. Resting on her heels, Savannah balanced herself with the arm of the chair so she could be eye-level with Penny, who remained curled up like a frightened kitten hiding from a predator.

"Pierce, I think."

"Do you know if he knew Dr. Sarong?"

"Uh huh."

"How did they know each other?"

"He was her boyfriend."

"Really?"

"Uh huh"

"Do you know anything else about him, like where he lived or worked?"

"Uh huh"

"What do you know about him?"

"I think he worked over there," she replied pointing out the window across Woodrow Wilson Drive.

"Do you mean he worked at Millsap College?"

"Uh huh"

"Do you know what he did at the college?"

"I think security or something."

"Thanks, Penny. Are you sure you are okay?"

"Uh huh"

"If you need anything, let me know, okay?" Savannah stood up to once again assess the situation.

"Okay," she replied and resumed her invisible posture.

Entering the doctor's private office, Savannah saw the body slumped back in the executive chair and blood covering the woman's chest. In the corner where her visitors sat in one of the arm chairs sprawled a once tall, African American male, a .38 hanging off his right hand and a hole in his temple with blood sprayed from the hole, down his cheek to the indigo and white pin-striped shirt.

"Gruesome," Doug said. "Apparently he shot her through the heart and turned the gun on himself. Just like the guy said—homicide—suicide."

"This is awful. But I was able to get some info out of Penny. So, I need you to run this down. According to her, this is Matthew Pierce and he works security at Millsaps and he was Sarong's boyfriend."

"Really? But she's from India."

"I know. And it appears their lives were worlds apart. But see what else you can find out."

"Okay. I'll see you back in the office."

"Savannah," called Andrew. "Come over here." The administrator directed her to the police detective, who had just arrived.

"Hi Savannah," greeted Lieutenant Paul Martin, a former member of Tom's SWAT team.

"Hi, Paul, so they sent you to investigate?"

"Well, that's where I am now—homicide. And this sure looks like a homicide to me. But it appears that the perpetrator has already taken care of the justice part. Did you know Dr. Sarong?"

"Just in a professional and ancillary manner. I did find out that this was a former boyfriend of hers. Maybe the former part was the reason for the shooting."

"Probably a love affair gone bad. Do you know if she has any relatives close by?"

"We are looking for that information now. She was from India and I think her family is still there. But our personnel records will show who her next of kin is. Do you want us to make that contact or you?"

"It might be best from you. But let me know if you have problems with it."

"Okay, but you'll handle Matthew Pierce, for sure?"

"For sure. We'll handle his notification. You said he works at Millsaps?"

"Yes, I think in security."

"Well, that explains why he had a .38 special. Most security guys carry these. I assume this was his gun, not hers. But we'll run that down, too."

"Paul, I'm sure the media will be here soon. Do you want to be the spokesperson? I think you can answer the questions better than I can, even though it is our hospital. I'm surprised they aren't here already. How did you get here so fast?"

"I was driving down Woodrow Wilson when the call came that shots had been fired at University Hospital. So, I took the call. Sure, I can speak to the media, but I won't have much to give them. Looks pretty open and shut to me. We'll notify Roger Thornton for the follow-up."

"Well, I'm glad you're here anyway and can talk to them. I'll see if we can get more info on Dr. Sarong for you," said Savannah, who knew Paul's quiet demeanor could dismantle even the most aggressive media. He was a big, soft-spoken guy and the right person to handle a potentially volatile situation.

An announcement over the hospital's system interrupted their conversation and paged Savannah to call her office immediately. She instinctively reached for Dr. Sarong's phone.

"Not that one," cautioned Paul. "This is still a crime area and we will be dusting for fingerprints. We don't need to find yours."

"Sure. I'll just use my cell."

"That would be better."

Savannah pulled her cell from her coat pocket and walked to a nearby window for better reception before she dialed her office. Certain places within the hospital prohibited cell phone reception and urology was one of them. Millie answered, but put her through to Doug immediately. Rummaging through Penny's desk Savannah found a notepad and pen to jot down details about Dr. Sarong from HR's file.

"Did you find out anything more about her former boyfriend?" she asked.

"Just that he has been working a Millsaps for ten years and was the superintendent for the campus security," explained Doug. "The guy I talked to has known Pierce for nearly ten years. But he was very private about his personal life, so he couldn't tell me anything about his relationship with Dr. Sarong. He said good things about him, like he was a great supervisor and cared about his people. Apparently, he had a temper. It took a lot to get him riled, but once he was, look out."

"Anything else?"

"That's about it. Just that my source said he was a big loss for Millsaps. He had come up through the ranks and earned a lot of respect."

"Okay. Have you had any media calls yet?"

"Yes, but I didn't give them anything because we don't have an official release yet. In my spare time I've been working on one."

"I talked to the homicide detective and he's going to take the lead on talking to the press, so just get the bare bones of what happened and then we'll refer them to JPD."

"Sounds good to me. By the way, your friend at Channel 3 wants you to call her."

"I'm sure she does. But it'll have to wait until I coordinate with Roger at JPD. When you get the release ready, call me back. I'm sure I'll still be here in urology. Talk to you later."

Dr. Pendleton, whose office was down the hall from Dr. Sarong, returned after examining the bodies and officially declared them both dead. It was obvious, but in a hospital, procedure still had to be followed.

"There's no doubt as to the cause of death of either of them—gunshot to the heart and to the temple. Probably only one shot to each, but an autopsy will confirm that. Have you called the coroner's office yet?" he asked.

"They are on the way," answered Paul. "Thanks for stepping in doc. We'll take it from here."

"I heard the gun shots as I was on my way to my office. So, I came in to see what I could do. But it was too late. Both shots were dead on. I was here almost immediately and still could not save either one. I went to Dr. Sarong first, but applying pressure to her chest didn't matter. You'd think a doctor in a hospital would make a difference," he said shaking his head. He still had blood on his hands and lab coat.

"Look, doc, it was right through the heart. You did what you could. One of the blue suits will get a signed statement from you later for our records."

"When do you guys want to address the media?" Andrew asked Paul and Savannah. "Hospital security corralled them downstairs in the lobby. But you know they won't be there long."

"Doug has a basic release we can read," remarked Savannah, "and you can take questions, Paul."

"Yeah, we might as well do this. Let's go."

Chapter 14

S takeouts were not Mitch's favorite part of his job, especially not like this one. Normally his telephoto lens clicked away at photos of spouses of his clients in compromising positions with someone of the opposite sex, other than their spouses. Tawdry escapades at least entertained his voyeuristic personality, but this indicated malfeasance and scared him. Twelve years on the police force had taught him a lot about people in general. They weren't what they appeared to be. They were like an onion, and peeling one layer off at a time would reveal the real substance, smelly parts and all.

Policemen were not above the law, but it went against Mitch's grain to think that a member of the police department where he had served would stoop so low. It wasn't that Mitch had been the perfect policeman, if he had been, he'd still be on the force. He just let his mouth and a love for liquor get him in trouble one too many times. But, this guy was one of the top rated guys, with heroic decorations and all. Why couldn't he have been on a competing team? Mitch mumbled and grumbled to himself as he snapped shots of the policeman meeting some guy in a dark suit at a dive on Lindsey Drive. At one time this was a night club owned by BJ Thomas, but had changed hands many times since then.

"So, who's the suit," he asked no one. The PI determined that he would find out who the man in the thousand dollar suit was because he appeared to be important. He did not recognize him, didn't remember his photo from the local papers, and had not heard scuttlebutt about him. He could only surmise that he owned or knew the owner of Cat Ballew. "What a weird name for a night club," he heard himself saying. "Whoa, I gotta quit this and spend more time with people who talk back."

They weren't hiding their meeting, so it couldn't be clandestine, just a suspicious, nocturnal encounter. Obviously they were unaware that anyone was interested in them or their little conference. Why would they? It could be a chance meeting of two old friends at a club and a conversation to catch up on life.

Mitch continued to watch the body language as their animated dialogue continued. The suit with a cigar in his hand kept pointing at the off-duty policeman and held a manila envelope in the other hand. Even from this distance the snoop knew his target wore Armani and the watch on his right hand was probably a Rolex. It all spelled money—big money. So when he passed the policeman a stuffed manila envelope that looked like a pay-off of some kind, it had to be a lot of dough.

The suspect accepted the envelope, but didn't appear to be happy about it. His brisk walk to the car parked at the far end of the club's parking indicated to Mitch that there was a problem. But the man in the suit strolled nonchalantly back into the dive.

The transaction was complete and captured on film. But it wasn't enough. Mitch needed more evidence. He needed to know why there was a pay-off, how much, and who was doing the paying? Did he follow the cop or the man in the suit? The man in the suit was easiest and may reveal more than following the policeman home, if that was where he was going.

Decisions, decisions. Mitch decided to try the night club. He could use a cold club soda anyway. The Indian summer heat was lingering too much this fall with the humidity in the nineties. Sweat drenched his face, often fogging up the viewfinder. His handkerchief was soaked from wiping his brow. He cranked up the window before setting foot out of the car, locked it, and made his way to the front door. Easy blues jazz on an alto saxophone from Billie Holliday's "Embraceable You" invited him in as he sauntered up to the bar made from Southern pine with a slate counter. Glasses hung from a ceiling rack and a wall-to-wall mirror stretched across the back so the bartender could see behind his back.

"Club soda on the rocks," he ordered. "Who's that on the sax?"

"He's George Hughes, the band teacher at Provine, but plays a mean sax. He was pretty much undiscovered until we had new management," explained the barkeep drying a long-stemmed glass, before filling Mitch's order.

"Well, it was quite a discovery and seems to have attracted a nice crowd. So you've got new management here? What can you tell me about him? Do you think he'll keep the place open?"

"I've been here off and on through about five owners and this guy seems to know how to manage," he replied setting down the soda in front of the patron. "He's from New

Orleans and he's paying me a lot more than I was making before. You see the crowd, well, this is a slow night. The weekends, it's packed."

"You don't say?" he sipped his drink. "What's this guy's name?"

"His name is Vinnie LaPresta and like I said he knows what he's doing. Why all the questions?"

"Just curious. I've seen this place start strong and then hit deep six many times. Wondering if it's gonna make it this time. What kind of name is LaPresta anyway?"

"I guess it's Italian. I don't know. I just work here."

"An Italian from New Orleans. Now that's an interesting combination."

Mitch turned on the swivel chair and listened to the soothing sounds of the sax, enjoying "All of You," "It Had to Be You," and some New Orleans style jazz before he left his payment and a handsome tip on the bar. He left with the basic information he was looking for. Tomorrow he'd have to investigate Mr. LaPresta and the policeman more. But that could wait. He wanted a good night's rest back at Morningside Apartments, an upscale complex off of North Jefferson Street in a quiet, older section of Jackson.

Early Saturday evening Mitch decided to check out Cat Ballew once again. Perhaps the new management would be available for a conversation with him. It wasn't even eight o'clock and he had to park on the street because the parking lot was completely full. Thronged with people he wondered if the fire marshal should be notified, but that would not endure him to the management, he thought as he slipped onto the only empty barstool he could find.

"Club soda," he ordered as he gauged the sea of people. Provine's band director was back on the sax, but joined with a bass, a soprano sax, piano player and a new guy on percussion. "Nice group," he told the bartender when his drink arrived.

"Yep, it attracts the crowd and they're all local."

"Makes it easy on the management if he doesn't have to go after them and pay is probably cheap."

"This is a second job for most of these guys, but they're good enough to play anywhere."

"Say, is Mr. LaPresta in?"

"Yeah, but he's in the office with some business partners."

"Really? I thought he owned the place."

"He does, but he owns several night clubs. One in Memphis, one in Atlanta, and of course one in New Orleans."

"He gets around, doesn't he?"

"Yeah, and if he comes out and catches me spending too much time with one customer, I'll be getting around, too."

"Sure, sure. Didn't mean to hold you up"

Mitch turned around to watch the crowd while he finished the club soda. He saw several members of the police force, all in civilian attire and having a good time. Some were dancing; some were just enjoying their companions. It looked like a place cops frequented and not too much to worry about. It could even explain why the plain clothes guy was talking to the owner.

"Mom, I'm so glad you're home," exclaimed Savannah into her phone.

"And where else would I be on Saturday night?"

"Oh, Mom, you know what I mean. I just need someone to talk to. It has been a really rough week with Dr. Sarong's murder."

"That must have been terrible, but at least they have the murderer."

"I guess that's the only good thing that came from it. The hospital has been a zoo with media and police traipsing in and out of urology. Surgeries were canceled and the department was basically off-limits."

"I read in the paper that he was a Black man. Wasn't she white and did that have anything to do with him shooting her?"

"Not really, and apparently race was not a factor. She was from India and didn't have any family in the U.S. I had to notify her parents and that was not easy. We didn't have a language barrier, but certainly a cultural one. They had no idea she had a boyfriend because according to their customs, she was supposed to come home in a month and marry someone from the western area of India where they live."

"Did that contribute to the problem with her boyfriend here?" her mom asked.

"Her parents are apparently very wealthy and do not permit marriage outside of their ethnicity. It is so strict that they forbid marriage to those from other parts of India. Can you imagine that? So you can imagine how shocked they were to hear how and by whom she was killed. I wish I had found out more about their culture before I called. Anyway, they will be here Monday to claim the body and take it back for cremation."

"Cremation?"

"Yes, they are Hindu and prefer cremation to burial. But the reason behind the shooting was she had broken off the engagement with Pierce. He had told one of his friends that, 'If I can't have her, then nobody can.' She was a beautiful woman, with her slender build, dark hair, dark skin and dark eyes. And she was brilliant."

"That's too bad. I'm sure her parents are distraught at losing their daughter."

"Yes, and now I'll be meeting with them Monday. We're even working through the State Department to make sure there are no glitches in transporting her body back to Mumbai. Changing the subject, my last visit with Tom Labor Day weekend seems eons ago. I wish he were still here so I could see him."

"I know you do. Have you heard anything from Barbara since your last encounter with her?"

"No, and I really haven't wanted to talk to her. My plate is full with work and rearranging schedules to see Tom. Lately we've had one crisis after another, and I barely have time to tread water."

"I know you love your job, but you really do need to find time for other things in life."

"I will. By the way, has Mr. Brown been able to find a loophole in that power of attorney? I've gotta find a way to bring Tom back. This is all too crazy."

"He hasn't done anything on it. I'm sorry, honey. I know you were counting on it, but he's really busy. I just can't push him right now."

"But, Mom."

"Just be patient. You know he's not charging for his services because you're my daughter. That's all we can do now. Just try to focus on something else—something fun for a change."

"Tomorrow after church Dee Dee and I are getting together for a tennis game at River Hills. It will be a time to let off steam and just have girl talk. Speaking of girl talk, have you heard from Lizzie?"

"Your sister is doing fine in California. She called last night for her weekly chat. She, Andy and the boys are planning to come home for Thanksgiving this year. You will be here, too, won't you?"

"I'll have to see what happens with Tom, before I can commit. But otherwise, I will be."

"Okay. I understand. It would be nice to have everyone together. Well, guess I'd better be off to bed now. Good night, sweetie. See you at church in the morning."

Savannah lay in bed, but couldn't sleep. She had an eerie sensation that something was wrong. The conversation she had with Mitch kept haunting her. Why had he been so interested in Chris and Pat? Chris he had known since high school and Pat was his former partner. Both men were close to Tom. It was strange that she would be thinking of this tonight instead of the murder. But there was no intrigue in the murder. It happened. It was horrible, but there was nothing to do about it. She just had to deal with the media—which of course would include her tennis game tomorrow. Yet, it was the questions about Chris and Pat that baffled her now, keeping her awake. Was there someone else involved? Who? He said there were other names on the list. What about the other teams? Was there something in her subconscious that she couldn't quite reach? Some detail of that day when Tom took his fall gnawed at her, but eluded her at the same time.

Chapter 15

Monday mornings were always busy for Anna Boone because Mr. Randall invariably conducted business on the golf course Saturday or at church on Sunday. Before he came to work he would call in with a list of items, cases, and briefs that needed reviewing or rewriting. And sometimes he would make appointments that weren't on his schedule. Despite her organizational skills and ability to multi-task with superb efficiency, Anna was blindsided by Barbara Whitehall.

"Where is he?" demanded Barbara as she brushed by Anna on her march to Dudley's office. Fortunately, it was locked forestalling her attack.

"Ma'am, he isn't due in the office until later. Do you have an appointment? I didn't see your name in the appointment book," Anna tried to smooth over the abruptness.

"I don't need an appointment. He'll see me."

"Yes, ma'am. I'm sure he will when he arrives, but meanwhile you are welcome to wait in the conference room."

"I'll wait out here, so I can see him when he comes in."

"May I get you a cup of coffee?" Anna offered, smiling to herself because she knew Mr. Randall would use his private entrance, rather than coming through the reception area. He would let her know when he was ready to see anyone.

"No, thanks. I'm fine."

Anna went through the conference room to put a note on Mr. Randall's desk that Mrs. Whitehall was waiting for him. Then she returned to her desk, trying to avoid eye contact with the pugnacious patron. She had plenty of work to do and being inspected by an intruder just gave her more incentive to intensify her efforts to keep busy. That way she didn't have to make small talk with her.

Fortunately Barbara found a magazine that captured her interest for the next hour or so. Whatever it was, Anna was grateful for distracting her boss' most cantankerous client. When Mr. Randall finally appeared from his office, his greeting surprised Barbara.

"Mrs. Whitehall, please come into my office and Anna, hold my calls," he requested.

In his private office, Dudley asked Barbara, "Please have a seat. Now, what can I do for you today?"

"I want to know what is holding up the paperwork appointing me guardian for Tom," asserted Barbara.

"I expected as much," he condescended as he pulled a file from his credenza. "Let me explain a few things first. I have the forms for you to sign, assigning you guardianship of Tom, but there are a couple of issues we need to discuss first. Tom does not have a will and there is no legal precedent for you to be his guardian, nor is there an example for appointing parents over the spouse as guardians. First, let me say that in 2006 there was a precedent set for establishing guardianship or conservatorship of an incapacitated person. In most cases this was necessary unless a prior power of attorney or living will existed and provided for conducting medical and business decisions that would be in the best interest of the individual or ward. At any rate, for the courts to agree with any action, it must be established to be in the best interest of the individual. While you do have a pre-existing power of attorney, it was prior to Tom's marriage. Since he never nullified it, the document remains legally binding. However, the law states:

> *For an individual who is incapable of making his/her own informed financial or health care decisions, and does not have any advanced directives in place, seeking guardianship is often the only way to ensure that the individual's best interest is promoted through sound decision-making. However, it is important for both the potential ward and the potential guardian to understand the benefits and drawbacks of establishing guardianship of an individual.*
>
> *Certain rights may not be exercised by a guardian without prior court approval on a case-by-case basis. These are: making a gift of the ward's money or property, selling the ward's real estate, transferring assets into a revocable trust, purchasing an insurance contract, making loans, and continuing any business that a ward previously conducted.*
>
> *Therefore, it is essential in cases where legal competency is in question to seek a professional determination before commencing the guardianship process. If an evaluator of a*

> *potential ward determines that the individual is*
> *competent to exercise legal authority on his/her*
> *own, the guardianship process can, and should,*
> *be avoided.*

"This means that we must have a doctor sign off on Tom's condition to proceed. Additionally, a court-appointed guardian ad-litem must be appointed to observe the potential ward and provide an objective opinion of the potential ward's competence. Then, in order to be appointed guardian, a formal court proceeding must take place, and the potential ward would have to make a court appearance. You will also need to gather substantial information for the court proceedings, including medical reports and a substantial amount of fact-finding paperwork.

"Now, having said that, one of the other issues is that to be a guardian, you must live in this state and the incapacitated person must also reside in the same state. That's where we have a problem with your son being in Georgia."

"What do you mean? Tom is in one of the best hospitals in the country. I don't want to move him and where would I move him?"

"It may be the best hospital and reflect the best interest of the individual, but it is in another state. That muddies the water for your guardianship, because you can't serve him best if he is in another state. Therefore, it means either you move to Georgia or you move him to Mississippi. Plain and simple. Second, I know that the University Hospital is one of the finest in the South and perhaps in the country when it comes to the new Rehab Center, but you will have to decide what you want to do, before you can sign these papers. Legally speaking, Tom's wife could just as easily petition the court for guardianship and nullify the previous power of attorney, if the court so rules. And if she wanted to, she could require him to be returned here."

"But that would cost money, which she doesn't have. And besides his father and I want what is best for him."

"Okay, but you will have to move him back if you want to proceed with this guardianship. Do you want to decide now or let me know later?"

"Let me see if there is any other place that will give him the care he needs first."

"You can do the research, but honestly, I don't think you will find a better rehab facility than the University."

"We'll see, Mr. Randall," she practically spewed at him. "We may look at the Baptist Medical Center."

"Check it out, but I don't think it has the rehab center that the University does."

"We shall see."

Barbara left spiriting an air of superiority to hide her feelings of disappointment and defeat. She just knew she would be able to keep Savannah away from Tom permanently. This was only the first step in her diabolical plan for a legal divorce. Now she had to make other arrangements for her plan to work. The bottom line for Barbara was to get rid of Savannah, who valued her career over marriage and had not produced any offspring. She had never liked the girl and these two reasons only fuelled the fire. She knew this turn of events for Tom was Savannah's fault. She should have encouraged Tom to pursue a football career like Billy Bob and Barbara wanted. Now she would have to pay.

At home she secluded herself in the study to make phone calls, the first to Billy Bob at his office, followed by calls to the rehab center in Atlanta and finally to the UMMC. It was settled, Tom could be moved back to Jackson by next week and Billy Bob would send the company jet for the trip. Barbara would fly down and oversee the transportation arrangements. She hoped to keep the operation clandestine to prevent Savannah's involvement, but mostly to keep her from making the trip. However, Billy Bob had other ideas.

Savannah exercised regularly at the hospital gym and then worked late most days to compensate for Tom's absence, so she was startled when her cell phone rang at nearly seven.

"This is Savannah Whitehall, how may I help you?"

"Savannah, this is Billy Bob. Did you know that we are going to move Tom back to UMMC next week?"

"What, really!" she could hardly believe her ears. "That's wonderful. Are you making the plans?"

"Yes, I am. In fact I'm using the company jet on Tuesday to go pick him up. Do you want to go with us?"

"Oh, I'd love to. How long will you be gone and what time will you be leaving?"

"Well, it will be a down and back on Tuesday. That's why I thought you might want to go. We'll leave from the Jackson airport around nine in the morning and if everything goes well, we should be back here no later than two o'clock. That way the University staff will be ready to move him into a private room."

"That's perfect. Shall I meet you at the airport at the private jet area about 8:30?"

"Yes, that will be fine and you might check with your doctor in charge of the rehab center."

"Certainly, Dr. Roddenburg is one of the best, if not the best in his field. He has really made some breakthroughs in his rehabilitation work with our neurologist and physical therapy. I know this will be great for Tom. It may even be the turning point for him. But I really appreciate your giving me a heads up on this so I can go. I was so disappointed when Tom was moved to Atlanta," she rambled in her excitement. "Thank you, thank you."

"I knew you'd want to know, Savannah. You take care now and I'll see you Tuesday. Okay?"

"Okay, and thanks again. Bye."

A grin exploded across Savannah's face as she contemplated the return of Tom. Now she could see him every day, check on his progress and know that he was being cared for by one of the best doctors in America. Work lost its luster as she stacked the reading materials on her desk. Going home just took on a new shape. Cleaning the house would be a priority—even though Tom wouldn't really be home. He would be closer and that meant more time for her to spend in his room.

Just at the thought of having Tom close by made Savannah's footsteps lighter. She practically danced to the car. Tomorrow she would ask Andrew Webster for a day off next week. She knew when she told him why, there would be no problem. The crispness of mid-October was invigorating with just enough chill to need a jacket. The oak and pecan trees that lined the back of the parking lot were visible in the sodium vapor security lights and displayed the ornamental gold, yellow and orange leaves as a gentle breeze caught them before they scattered on the ground below.

Savannah remembered reading somewhere that it was not the wind that causes the leaves to fall, but a message from the tree's system tells the branch when to let go of the leaves. That's why some trees hang on to their leaves, while others seem to drop all the leaves at once. Nonetheless, watching the process was like watching the hand of the Master as He painted the masterpiece of the universe for His greatest creation—mankind.

In her moment of elation, Savannah's heart skipped a beat. Was she being watched? She felt ominous eyes following her every move.

Chapter 16

itch scheduled an appointment with Chief Bennett for the following morning. This would not be pleasant and he knew he had better have his facts straight. Bennett was not a man to play games and he was a big protector of his department. But right now he had another matter to take care of.

"Mrs. Whitehall," he said.

Savannah nearly jumped out of her skin at the sound of Mitch's voice. She had not seen anyone around the parking lot and he seemed to appear out of thin air.

"Mitch Adams, where did you come from?"

"I'm sorry, I didn't mean to startle you, but I need to verify some information with you and I don't want to put you in any danger. It is not safe to meet you in public—at least for you."

"What do you mean, not safe? You could have come to my office for a meeting. We could have met privately, not out here."

"That's just it. The more I find out, the more danger I find, especially for you."

"For me?"

"Well, as I told you before, Tom's fall was no accident. It was sabotage and there seems to be more to it than just winning a competition. But I really don't want to get into that right now and the less you know, the better it will be for you. So, what I need from you right now is any information you might have heard about cases Tom was working on. Something about a drug bust?"

"Tom and I talked a lot, but when it came to his work, there were very few details he would give me—at least until it was all wrapped up. So, if you are talking about a case he was working on before the accident, I wouldn't have any details at all."

"Did he ever mention going to a joint called Cat Ballew?"

"Mmmm, that sounds vaguely familiar, but not sure why."

"It's a nightclub on Lindsey Drive near Robinson Road. He might have been on a stakeout there or been a part of a drug raid."

"I do seem to recall a case he worked maybe a year or so ago when he told me about a big drug bust. But, gee, that was a long time ago."

"Do you know if he was working with Pat O'Brien or Chris O'Donnell or one of the other SWAT guys at the time?"

"He could have. I think that's the last time he and Chris worked together was before Chris left SWAT for IA. I seem to remember that it was a big raid and lots of people taken to jail and a photo on the front page of the *Clarion-Ledger*. It may be the newspaper article that I remember the most. But you know, it could just as easily have been Pat or someone else. Like I said, he doesn't read me into his cases. So, I'm not much help there. Sorry."

"That helps me anyway. Thanks, I appreciate it," he said tipping his head.

"You're welcome. But next time, couldn't you call first instead of scaring the bejeebers out of me?"

"I'm really sorry about that, but I don't want anyone to know I'm talking to you. It is for your own good, really."

"Okay, okay. Oh and Tom's going to be moved back here to the hospital next week. See ya."

Savannah slid into her bucket seat and started the motor, with her hands still trembling. She kept assuring herself that it was only Mitch who had been watching her. But why did he keep warning her about how dangerous their meeting was? Just something else to ponder on the drive home. She cranked up the radio with "Sugar, Sugar, you are my candy girl," diverting her attention.

Mitch concentrated on his line of questions for his new friend during the drive to Cat Ballew. Vinnie was debonair, but in a creepy way. He could have stepped out the *Godfather* with his slick, black hair and a hint of Italian and New Orleans accent. Like the bartender told him, he was smart—street smart and an intellectual—a scary combination. But Mitch had managed to cozy up with him through his frequent visits to the new jazz club. It suited him fine because jazz was his kind of music and made this part of the job more enjoyable.

"Hey, Vinnie, my man, how goes it?" Mitch asked as he cut through the smoke and found his contact at a corner table near the bar.

"Pull up a chair and take a load off," replied Vinnie through teeth that clenched a stogie.

"Looks like a great crowd for Thursday night."

"Yeah, this saxophone guy really has been drawing them in. I may have to raise his pay, you know."

"Is it a usual group or do you get quite a lot of new people?"

"Oh, you know there are some regulars, especially for Thursday nights, but then we get a few new ones straggling in. Maybe the word is getting out. But Sunday nights are really slow. I guess too many who have to be at work Monday morning and don't want the Monday hangover."

"Yeah, I suppose so for those with regular jobs. But your band director doesn't play on Sundays, does he?"

"Nope, he doesn't. You got a point there."

"This place used to have a bad reputation, but since you've been here, things have changed. Looks like you cleaned it up a lot."

"You might say that. But it doesn't hurt to have friends with the JPD, either," Vinnie grinned sheepishly. He always sat with his back to the wall.

"Yep, that would help keep things humming."

"Did you come to chat or drink?" Vinnie asked as a waitress in a white blouse with a short black skirt and dark hose approached the table.

"A little of both. Club soda on the rocks," he ordered eyeing the voluptuous server.

"Enjoy, I need to get to work. Paper work never seems to end," said Vinnie as he rose to leave. He headed around the bar to his backroom office.

Adjusting his chair to put his back to the wall, Mitch wanted a better view of the patrons without being too obvious. His friend had inadvertently answered unasked questions. It was still early, but some observations of the cliental would help him with his meeting with the chief.

"Good morning, Judy," Mitch greeted Chief Bennett's secretary as he gently closed the hallway door behind him. "Is he in?" he nodded toward the chief's door.

"Good morning, Mr. Adams," she replied. "Yes, he is. I'll let him know you are here." She buzzed the intercom, "Mr. Adams is here for his appointment."

"Thank you, Judy. Send him in, please," replied the intercom speaker on the phone.

"Nice to see you, Mitch. Have a seat. What have you got for me?"

"Nice to see you, too. But what I have isn't so nice. Let me lay it out on the table for you. You know the new club called Cat Ballew?"

"Yeah. It used to be called BJ's and the Lighter Side and something else with lots of trouble there. But it seems to have quieted down under the new management."

"You could say that. But the truth is the new owner has some of your people on his payroll."

"You're kidding me? Who?"

"What I can say right now is for you to take a hard look at Internal Affairs investigations. I think they are investigating the corruption, and I might know who, but it is only a supposition. No proof yet."

"Okay, I'll look into that. But don't share this info with anyone else, at least until I have time to check it out. Got it?"

"Sure. One more thing. It looks like the new management at the club and what happened to Tom Whitehall are connected. The same person's name keeps coming up on both counts. But again, I haven't connected all the dots. I just want you to know this because it appears that my investigation is getting dicey, even for me. Take a look at these photos I took about a month ago."

"This is at Cat Ballew?"

"Yep. This was before I got the connection. I've been spending some time there listening to some great jazz, but there are others getting jazzed there, too. If you know what I mean."

"But this is one of my key guys exchanging envelopes with the man in the dark grey suit. Who is he?"

"The grey suit is Vinnie LaPresta, the owner and a well-connected guy from New Orleans. Unless you have some sort of sting operation in process, this makes your guy a bad cop. But that's not the only time I've witnessed these two exchanging packages at the club. This just happens to be the only time I took a picture. I'm working on Tom's case and this is just added attractions to the investigation."

"But you said it had some connection with Tom?"

"Yeah, but not all the dots are in line yet. I just want you to be aware and just in case anything happens to me, you'll have a place to start looking."

"I appreciate the heads up and will do some looking myself, but as you know, we need to keep this between the two of us. Anyone else on the force you're looking at?"

"There is someone else, but I don't have enough on him. I just hope he's the only one. I still think the JPD has honest people. By the way, did you know Tom will be moved back to Jackson?"

"No, I haven't heard that. How did you find out?"

"His wife told me last night."

"You saw his wife last night?" he exclaimed with disdain.

"Yeah, yeah. Don't get all excited. I needed to ask her some questions, so I waited for her in the hospital parking lot. She's been helpful in lining up some of the dots in this case."

"Okay. But let's keep her out of it as much as possible. Got it?"

"Yeah, sure. Let me know if you find out anything else other than what I gave you and I will likewise."

"Okay, Mitch. Take it easy."

Mitch ambled out the door dwelling on how he could find hard evidence of what these two were up to. He knew Tom must have had some inside information and that was why he had been injured. The PI had a hunch that the accident should have been fatal, but Tom's top-notch condition had made him a survivor.

He had work to do. It was a good thing Mr. Whitehall was paying him for his time and expenses because the legwork on this case prevented him from taking on any other cases—especially his favorites—divorces, which were his bread and butter as well as giving him extensive opportunities for prurience and using his Nikon digital-telephoto lens camera. However, there were other perks to this case, like the intrigue as well as malevolence it personified with his former brothers in blue. This was the kind of case that he would work for free, if he had to. But he didn't. And that was the best part—his boss was wealthy and paid him well.

Chapter 17

r. Roddenburg met Savannah, Tom, his parents and the attending nurse at the entrance of the rehab center. He personally wanted to supervise and assess Tom's vitals and functionality. This was his area of expertise, his research project and study as well as his tangential personal interest.

Savannah was relieved to have Tom back at UMMC and with Roddenburg tending to his physical well-being. This was an answer to her prayers. However, the trip had been anything but happy. If looks could kill, both she and Billy Bob would have been dead. He neglected to tell Barbara that Savannah would meet them at the airport and sparks flew when she walked into the private aircraft terminal.

"What is she doing here?" Barbara yelled so loudly that everyone in the hangar stopped to look.

"Honey, I forgot to tell you that I invited her yesterday. We've been so busy getting ready for the trip. And you know she works for the hospital, so I thought it reasonable for her to bring him back."

"Well, I don't. And you didn't consult me on this at all."

"I'm sorry, sweetie. I've been so busy with all the arrangements. You know how it is. And besides, she is his wife. It is proper that she be here. Wouldn't you be there for me?"

"I guess since she's here, she can go," Barbara acquiesced.

When they arrived at UMMC, Barbara announced, "I will stay with Tom until all the tests are run."

"Thank you, Barbara and Billy Bob for letting me go with you. I do have some work to catch up on, so I'll see you later," Savannah said excusing herself from any more confrontations with Barbara. A formidable foe for friends or family, Barbara was not to be tangled with. What she lacked in physical size, her disposition and presence made up for it. Billy Bob was probably the only person, other than her own mother, who could manage her.

Undaunted by her mother-in-law's icy attitude, Savannah returned to her office early with a song in her heart and a new lease on life. As she rummaged through the files on her desk, she saw a list of questions from Dee Dee about Dr. Sarong. A month ago Dr. Sarong was murdered, but the shock still lingered in the hallways of the hospital with whispered conversations. However, WLBT wanted to do a feature on the doctor from India.

Thinking about all the lives of the people she saw every day, Savannah recalled a not so serious comment from a co-worker when she first began working at UMMC. It was a large hospital and her acquaintance said it was like any of the soap operas on daytime TV, especially *General Hospital*. There were always crises, either personal or by the virtue of its mission. Just like in *General Hospital* the people's lives in and out of the complex touched so many lives throughout the state and now around the world. Dr. Sarong's untimely death was a tragedy affecting many lives, but a romance gone bad imparted an ironic twist straight from the pages of a soap script. Her Indian background heightened awareness of cultural differences and created international interest.

Dialing her friend's cell number, Savannah drummed her pen on the pad with Dee Dee's questions. Prepared with the basic answers to the queries, she knew her friend would naturally be provoked to probe into more subtle situations. There was one question Dee Dee always asked and she couldn't wait to answer it. Dee Dee could share her joy when she passed on the news about Tom. That was the real story of the day—and with Dr. Roddenburg in charge of Tom's care, she was ecstatic.

"Hello, Dee Dee. I've got some great news to pass on to you!" she exclaimed.

"Really? You have insight into the relationship between Sarong and Pierce?"

"No, no. But this is even better. Tom is back at UMMC. I came back with him today."

"That is great news. But why aren't you with him right now? Sarong's story can wait—it's not breaking news now."

"His mom's with him now and they are in the rehab center. Our head doc has been making inroads with that car wreck victim and now he can start working with Tom. This could be just the path that leads Tom to recovery."

"I understand, but don't get your hopes too high. From what you've told me, Tom has a long way to go."

"I know, I know. But I can still hope and I do have lots of hope for him."

"The eternal optimist, as always, Savannah. You never cease to amaze me. I guess that's why you went into PR and I stayed with investigative reporting to sniff out the bad. Speaking of bad, what do you have for me on Sarong and Pierce?"

Miles away in downtown Jackson, Mitch arrived at Chief Bennett's office once again with photos and a stack of papers.

"I connected the dots," Mitch said triumphantly. "And here they are."

Mulling over the photos, the chief clearly identified one of his officers with Vinnie LaPresta counting money in one envelope and yet another package wrapped in brown paper.

"This is basically what you had before, Mitch. But it isn't enough."

"Ah, but I also have a recording of their conversation. The sad thing is that my favorite sax player is involved. On this little thumb drive, we have Vinnie and a JPD person making their deal and talking about George Hughes as their rep to the kids. I guess a teacher's salary just wasn't enough for him and the temptation of having an easy mark at school was too much.

"But that's not all. I have a buddy that runs a machine shop and he examined the bar that brought down Tom Whitehall. According to him, it had been sawed nearly in two before Tom ever touched it. It would take a very special saw to penetrate that metal bar and that kind of saw can't be purchased just anywhere. Only places that sell specialized farm tools or saws used in manufacturing would have one. There's only one place in Rankin or Hinds County that sells them—Jack's Tool Shed in Terry. So, I visited Jack's Tool

Shed and found out that he sold one on March 15 to this guy. Beware the ides of March."

"I don't suppose you have a copy of that sales receipt in this stack somewhere?"

"As a matter of fact, I do," Mitch beamed as he pulled a quarter sheet of paper from the stack, like a magician pulling a rabbit out of a hat. Assembling his findings out on the chief's rather clean desktop gave him a sense of pride of a job well-done.

"Like I said, there aren't many of these saws sold around here and old Jack remembers the sale as if it were yesterday. He said this tall blond-headed guy comes in giving him a song and dance about building a homemade swing set with galvanized steel rods. So he needs this special saw to cut the 10-foot rods he's using. I mean, Jack went on and on about the guy's story. He said it didn't track with him, but he let the guy spill his guts. So, he identified your guy from one of my photos and then he had the sales slip, too. You would have thought he'd made up a name and paid in cash, but, no he used a credit card. And you know what, Jack keeps unbelievable records. Said he was audited by the IRS one time and doesn't want that to happen again. But we got him with the saw."

"This is great, Mitch, but we've got to put him there doing it. And prove his motive—which is?"

"This part is harder to prove. But apparently, on one of the raids when Cat Ballew was still under the former management, Tom was a part of the SWAT team that went in. What I've been able to piece together is that this officer was not part of the raiding party but suddenly appeared on the scene. Tom became suspicious and that's where my info falls short. If Tom were here, he could finish this scenario for us. That's why I think he's in a coma. He wasn't supposed to live. That bar was 10 feet high and with the momentum needed to swing from it to the next bar, the impact should have been fatal. It was certainly attempted murder. So, what do you think—enough to make an arrest?"

"It's a good case. I'll take it to the D.A. and see what he says. We do have to walk softly on this. So, until I give the word, keep it to yourself, okay?"

"Sure, boss."

"What's your angle on all this anyway?"

"I have a well-paying client whose interest is in Tom, not the drug bust or the other characters. So, I want to keep a low profile on this one anyway."

Mitch left the JPD headquarters feeling like he'd just climbed Mt. Everest. This case was working out well for him. He started out watching Savannah Whitehall—not really much to watch since her days were spent at the office and her nights at home—and then the case turned juicy. Real detective work. That was what he was doing now, but he didn't want to be party to the drug activities. Vinnie and his pals were out of his league, and he knew it. The quicker he could pass that on, the better he felt. His job was watching other people, but with this he felt like the watched, not the watcher.

Two days later Mitch picked up the *Clarion-Ledger* from his doorstep and read the headlines—*Drug Lord, Local Policeman Arrested*. There were Vinnie and the cop in handcuffs with their heads hanging down trying to avoid being photographed. He scanned the story. Nothing mentioned him or any specific sources in the arrest. He felt safe. At least he could still walk the streets without looking over his shoulder. He failed to notice the strange car parked in the apartment parking lot with two people in it.

Chapter 18

"Good morning," Barbara greeted Anna arrogantly. "Is he in?" she asked peering down the hall to the open door.

"Yes, Mrs. Whitehall. He is expecting you. Please go in."

"All right, Mr. Randall, Tom has been back in Jackson three weeks and we need to get on with this process. Do you have the legal forms ready making me his guardian?"

"Yes, ma'am. They are right here. But I thought it was for both you and Mr. Whitehall."

"No, it is just me. He just gets to pay for it all. That's the arrangement we have. He makes the money and I get to spend it. It's kept us happy for 35 years."

"I see," Dudley condescended looking away from his client and reaching for other papers in her file. A tall-lanky man who always wore a three-piece suit, he portrayed professionalism even when conducting disgusting deals like this that made him nauseous. But she was the client and he did his best to keep the process legal, even if it wasn't the moral thing to do. Ethics he could debate with the best of them, but with a bull-headed battleax, it was futile.

"Now what have you done about a law suit against the police department?"

"Well, I am working on it"

Dudley had other clients, but as far as Barbara was concerned, she was it. And the Whitehalls kept him very busy with a variety of legal matters including the car dealerships as well as personal matters.

"We will have to find evidence of an intention to injure," he explained. "What is your purpose in filing such action? Is it to be monetarily compensated or to indicate negligence within the department?"

"I think we should go for both. Those medical bills are certainly piling up and my boy wouldn't be in the hospital if they had not been negligent in checking the equipment. I still don't see how this happened at a police training site."

"Don't you have a private eye investigating this? What does he say?"

"Billy Bob and he have been discussing this issue, so I don't have the particulars of the situation. I just know there's a policemen that they think is responsible for his fall."

"What's the name of the PI, so I can get the details from him?"

"You better talk to Billy Bob about that. I don't remember his name. I met him only once and don't really have any contact with him."

"Okay. Now if you'll just sign these papers right here." Rising from his desk, he stepped into the hallway and called, "Anna, could you come in and notarize Mrs. Whitehall's signature, please?"

"How long will the civil suit take?"

"It could drag out for a couple of years, depending on how much evidence we have and if the police department decides to settle out of court or not. There are lots of variables, some depending on the judge assigned to the case and whether or not we pursue a criminal or civil case."

"Well, it was criminal, wasn't it?"

"Yes, but in criminal cases you have to prove beyond a shadow of a doubt, but if it is civil, we just have to show intent to harm."

"Oh, I see. Well, I'll leave all the legal mumbo-jumbo up to you and Billy Bob. I'm just looking out for my son."

"I will file these guardianship papers at the courthouse this week, but the authorization won't take place until they are registered and returned."

"I had no idea all of this would take so long and then we still have to file for a divorce on Tom's behalf. Will we still be able to use the abandonment clause?"

"It will be difficult to say the least, but the longer he is in the hospital, the more veritable we can make it, the better chance of success we'll have. It all takes time."

Barbara left the warm, plush law offices somewhat satisfied. At least the plan to prohibit Savannah from making claims to Tom's future inheritance or overseeing his medical treatment was put into motion. She was worse than a mad momma bear losing her cubs when it came to protecting her sons, especially her baby boy. Unfortunately, her actions often resembled those of a wild animal, untamed and unrelenting in her pursuit without regard to consequences.

Thanksgiving plans and food preparation were underway for Savannah, Elizabeth and their mom, who had already decided on the menu and assigned tasks for the day. Liz, Andy, and the boys flew in from California on Wednesday and planned to stay at her mom's until Monday morning. Liz was there to help her mom cook the turkey and dressing while Andy entertained the boys.

Elizabeth earned an associate's degree in computer design at Hinds Junior College before marrying Andrew Jenkins, a computer engineer, and moving to San Jose. Now Lizzie had Andy Jr. and Bryan, one named for his dad and the other named for his granddad. The boys kept Liz busy as a stay-at-home mom.

Savannah completed the Canfield traditional meal with her pecan pie and green bean casserole. Family was important to the Canfields and it would not be the same without Tom there to celebrate, but tomorrow the youngest daughter could stop by the hospital in the morning on the way to her mom's. The pie and the casserole baked in the oven while Savannah stirred together the ingredients for the fruit salad, a recipe given to her by Wanda when they had a potluck at the office two years ago. Every time she made it, she would think of Wanda and how she missed her efficiency and generous smile.

The last year had taken a toll on the young woman, who felt she had aged ten years. Her losses were not tangible material things, like in a major disaster, but those with intrinsic value. Wanda's death had been a blow to Savannah both professionally and personally, because she had depended on her assistant to run her daily life. Even though Millie's competence mirrored Wanda's, there had been a special bond between her and Wanda that was unexplainable. It wasn't fair to compare Millie to Wanda, they were entirely different people. But yet, the loss of a friend changed the dynamics of the relationship of boss and employee.

When it came to thinking about Tom, the penetrating pain prevented her from articulating the ache within the core of her essence. Yes, Tom was still alive and she still had the expectation of his full recovery one day. But as the days had stretched into months, that dream diminished into a dismal doubt. However, Thanksgiving was a time to give thanks for what one had, not what one did not have. Tom was still alive and for that she was thankful.

Savannah pulled into the driveway of the small red-brick home on Peachtree Drive, where tall southern pines lined the street and privet hedges divided neighbors' yards. Bright yellow and gold chrysanthemums, untouched by the frost from the brisk morning, graced the flower bed under the living room window and greeted visitors. Although she didn't consider herself a visitor, Savannah still rang the doorbell before entering. Liz greeted her with a big hug, almost causing her drop the pie.

"Hello, little sis. It is so good to see you. You look wonderful. Here let me take that," said Liz all in one gasp.

"Liz, it's good to see you, too. Let me get the rest of the food from the car before I freeze to death," she replied before running back to get the casserole and salad out of the trunk.

Andy stood at the door holding it open for his sister-in-law, "We've been waiting for you," he teased.

"Glad you didn't start without me," Savannah muffled as she hugged him with one arm after he took the salad from her.

Andy closed the front door and two young boys ran into the living room to greet Aunt Savannah, yelling, "Aunt Susie, Aunt Susie."

Savannah was a mouthful for anyone, let alone boys aged 5 and 3. After grabbing her legs, they followed her into the dining room, which faced the covered patio and the backyard partially covered with pine needles and dotted by pine cones. It was perfectly landscaped with a gazebo in place of the metal swing set the girls had played on growing up. Around the gazebo were the azalea and lilac bushes that in the spring would be covered in fuchsia and lavender stars and a wisteria vine devoid of leaves wrapped itself around the entrance. The rose garden under her mother's bedroom window was nothing but sticks with thorns. It too would come to life in the spring and fill the yard and the house with the sweet aroma of pink, burgundy, and salmon roses. Even looking at the bleakness of winter, one could see hope that would come in the spring.

"Mom, the table looks wonderful," commented the new arrival. "The Rosemont china looks beautiful with the green and gold tablecloth. And I love the little ceramic turkeys. We have had them on the table for as long as I can remember."

"Yes, your dad bought them the second year we were married," she replied. "It was the first year I cooked our Thanksgiving meal. Our first year we went to my mom's for Thanksgiving. He wanted that year to be so special and it was. When I cooked the turkey, I removed the giblets from the inside of the turkey, but didn't know there was another bag with the neck bone in that cavity. What a surprise it was when he started carving the turkey!"

"Oh, mom, I can't believe you did that," exclaimed Liz. "I don't think you ever told us that story before."

"Well, it was not one of my favorites and your dad certainly wouldn't tell it. He was always so considerate of my feelings, and he didn't want anything to make me look bad. You know he never allowed anyone to speak harshly to or about 'the woman I love'. I can still hear him saying that."

"Me, too, mom."

"How long before we eat?" asked Andy interrupting the trip down memory lane. "I've smelled the turkey all morning and I'm famished."

"Me, too," exclaimed Andy Jr.

"Me, three," said Bryan.

"You're always famished," commented Liz with a smile. "If you didn't work out all the time, you'd be as big as a barn."

"Ah, but that's my secret—working out. Can't let Tom be the only one who stays fit as a fiddle. Speaking of Tom, how is he, Savannah?"

"Now that he is back under Dr. Roddenburg's care, I think we will see some improvements very soon. Dr. Roddenburg has developed a mechanical physical therapist that exercises Tom's arms and legs on a regular basis. It also measures the atrophy of his muscles to determine the tension to put on them. Keeping him mechanically active is one way of maintaining the homeostasis for his bodily functions. Additionally, Dr. Pendleton monitors his neurological activity through electrodes, which indicate a near normal rate. So the prognosis is good, but he's still catatonic. That's why I'm so grateful for having him here at the hospital so I can visit him daily."

Mary Ann brought in the turkey on the Rosemont platter, placing it between the two ceramic turkeys and completing the table setting with enough food to feed an entire platoon. Thanksgiving was about feasting, family and football at the Canfield house.

"Andy, as the man of the house today, you have the honor of returning thanks and carving the turkey," announced Mary Ann.

"I'd be pleased to do both," he replied bowing his head. "Lord, for this great bounty we are grateful. For your love and the love in this family, we are grateful. May we always remember that all of this comes as your gift to us. And for your Son, Jesus, we are eternally grateful that He, too, brings the gift of salvation. Bless this food, this house, and all of our family. In Your Son's name we pray. Amen. And dig in!" he added as he picked up the electric knife and the meat fork.

"So, Susie, what do you do when you visit Tom?" asked Liz. "Do you just sit there?"

"Well, I do sit there, but I also read to him. I stroke his face and hands. And I just talk to him. Dr. Pendleton says that somewhere in his unconsciousness he hears me and he can tell from the print outs when I have been to see Tom."

"Really? It makes that much difference?" asked Andy.

"Yes, the amount of brain activity increases and on a subconscious level he seems to respond. In fact, since he has been moved back here, there have been distinctive improvements from those recorded by Dr. Cummings in Atlanta."

"I had no idea Tom was doing this well," remarked Liz. "This is great news."

"Yes, I am so thankful that the Whitehalls brought him back. I believe that Tom could make a full recovery. You see, his body has healed from the fall. The broken bones have been restored. With the physical therapy his muscles are exercising and gaining strength, maybe not what he was, but at least some. If he will wake up, then there is a prognosis that he can fully recover."

"So, why doesn't he wake up?" asked Andy.

"Dr. Pendleton says it has to do with the shock his body experienced during the impact. The trauma was so intense that he shut down to endure the pain. Now that physically he's healed, it will still take time for his brain to recognize it. But from the brain fluctuations it is apparent that it is responding. He could wake up any day or never. I choose to think it will be someday soon."

"We will continue to pray for him, Savannah," her mom assured her.

After the meal Liz put the boys down for a nap and went to find her little sister. "Susie, tell me how things are going for you. It must be so hard with Tom in a coma and all the other things you have going on. Mom has kept me informed about the major things, but what about day to day?" she asked as the two girls settled on the living room sofa that had occupied the wall across from the picture window for 30 years. It was a formal sitting area that had been off-limits when they were growing up. But today it was a respite for them.

Taking her shoes off and resting her feet on the oblong cherry coffee table with a glass inlay, Savannah leaned her head back on the cushion. "I have reflected on this year many times, looking at the changes that have overwhelmed me and I just can't imagine getting through it all without mom. I don't know how she managed when dad died and we were so young. Yet I realize how God has been the stalwart for her and for me."

"I guess it's like she always says," mused Liz, "God is in control and all things do work together for them that love the Lord. I just can't imagine if anything happened to Andy. How would I raise the boys by myself? I know it's different for you because you don't have kids, but then you go home to an empty home. What's that like for you?"

"You know, I just have to keep counting my blessings. Yes, Tom is in a coma, but he didn't die, like dad did. So, it isn't forever and I still have the possibility for him to come back. And I have my work that has been an incredible series of ups and downs."

"Yeah, tell me about that. Who was that doctor that got shot?"

"That was an awful day. Dr. Sarong was a beautiful, intelligent urologist from India and a very private person. The shooting blind-sided everyone, including her family. They came from India to take her body back for cremation. It was my first time to deal with a Hindu family. They were very soft spoken, but had very specific instructions for her body. I'll never forget walking into Sarong's office and seeing the blood from both of their wounds. You know I have been in ER and seen lots of blood and guts, but this was different."

"How so?"

"Well, she was someone I knew and it was personal. I guess like it was when I found out Wanda had died in the tornado. It was different for me. I deal with disasters and crises. I prepare for them and help train others to be ready for them. But when it's someone close, it takes it to another level. It's hard to be objective and to maintain a neutral position when it's personal. You can rationalize anything, but where is the justice? I suppose the fact that Sarong's significant other took his own life was some sort of justice. But where is the justice in Tom's condition? Someone deliberately cut that bar causing his injuries. As of yet, I don't know who did it."

"Wait. It wasn't an accident?"

"Not according to a PI investigating it," Savannah replied sitting up with her feet back on the floor. "And it may have been someone close to Tom."

"Mom didn't tell me that," Liz said turning to her sister with her left arm akimbo.

"Well, she wasn't supposed to discuss it because it is ongoing. Neither am I, but I know you won't tell anyone."

"There you are," announced Andy. "I was wondering where the girls are. How about an after dinner walk?"

"We'll have to finish this discussion later," said Liz as she and Andy retrieved their jackets from the foyer closet.

Chapter 19

A week after Thanksgiving Dudley called the Whitehall home and left a message with the maid for Barbara to come to his office.

Barbara was getting ready for a Christmas shopping trip to the mall when Pearl knocked on the door of the master suite.

"Yes, what is it?" grunted Barbara annoyed with being disturbed.

"Excuse me, Mrs. Whitehall, but Mr. Randall called to say that the guardianship papers had been returned from the court."

"Really? And why didn't you let me speak to him?" she yelled through the door.

"I could hear the shower running and he just asked me to give you the message, ma'am."

"Okay, okay. That'll be all," she replied and began grumbling to herself as she finished dressing.

Pearl scurried away avoiding any more contact with her boss. She knew her boss' mood would change on a dime with information like this and she didn't want to be in the line of sight in case there were any missiles fired. For more than 20 years Pearl had been a part of the Whitehall household. She had her own suite on the first floor next to the kitchen. It was her retreat when Mrs. Whitehall was on the warpath. Pearl normally ran the household, but she also knew how to become scarce.

Actually Barbara was pleased with the thought of the paperwork being ready for her to sign. She made a beeline to the lawyer's office, and would do her planned shopping afterwards as a celebration. Spending Billy Bob's money on gifts would heighten her sense of satisfaction and generosity—not always her best side. But today was special. She was on her way to transforming an abhorrent event into a coup, thanks to her husband's lawyer.

"It's about time," she stormed at Dudley. "This does mean that I am now officially his guardian?"

"Yes, ma'am, it does."

"Now, what about the divorce proceedings? Can we move forward with them?"

"Not so fast, Mrs. Whitehall. We filed the papers at the end of September and it takes six months before it is final. And it can be contested during that time or become null and void by the members of the marriage."

"But it has to be agreed by both parties, right?"

"That is correct."

"And I represent one of the parties, correct?"

"That is also correct."

"So, if I do not agree to reconcile or stop the divorce, then it will be final six months from the date of filing, right?"

"That is right."

"So as long as things are status quo, the divorce will be final in March?"

"Right again."

"Now back to the guardianship papers, just what do they authorize me to do on Tom's behalf?"

"Well, you can make decisions about his medical and physical care as long as they are in the best interest of the person you are representing. If you make a decision that does not appear to be for his best interest, it can be challenged in court. What do you have in mind?"

"The house his wife lives in was purchased in part with money from my husband. Since Tom can no longer reside there, I want to have her evicted. Can I as his guardian evict her?"

"You want to do what?" He could not believe his ears. This was certainly a new twist to the most bizarre case he'd ever filed.

"Evict her. Kick her out of the house and take it back."

"Whatever for?"

"Because my husband spent money on that place and this is just one more step to keep her out of Tom's life."

"You are unbelievable. Was the house completely paid for by your husband?"

"Well, not all of it. Just the down payment, which was substantial."

"So who makes payments now?"

"Tom did while he was working, but he's not drawing a salary right now."

"So she is making the payments?"

"Well, I guess."

"And the bank holds the mortgage, right?"

"Yes, but what's that got to do with it?"

"Well, whose name or names are on the mortgage?"

"Tom and Savannah."

"Then you can't evict her."

"But what if I represent Tom's case?"

"Okay, I see your point, but I'm not sure that this will work. Let me research it some more before we serve her an eviction notice."

"But what do I need to do to request she be served a notice?"

"You have to provide proof of ownership and stipulate a cause for eviction, which is normally a lack of payment. And right now you can't. Besides after serving notice, depending on how long it has been since a payment was made, the person can make the required payment and forestall the eviction."

"But just to serve the notice, do you have to prove all that?"

"No, you can have the constable serve the papers, but the person can contest them if there isn't just cause."

"Then that's what I want to do."

"Wait a minute. Does Mr. Whitehall know you are doing this?"

"What does that matter?"

"Like you said, it is his money. He should be aware of what you are doing."

"Maybe he does and maybe he doesn't. Just draw up the papers."

"Don't you realize Christmas is just around the corner? Why would you want to evict someone just before Christmas?"

"It would be harder to protest during the holidays wouldn't it?"

"Some of the judges won't hear new cases during the holidays. They just want to clear their dockets. But she wouldn't have to get out until January. No constable will enforce an eviction during the holidays. So, what's the rush?"

"I just want to make a point."

"It'll make a point all right," he mumbled. What he didn't say was how he thought that she was just a mean-spirited person. It was incredulous to him that anyone could be so heartless.

"So, you'll do it?"

"I'll look into it, Mrs. Whitehall."

When Barbara opened the door to the hallway, the soft instrumental sounds of "We Wish You a Merry Christmas" wafted through the office.

"Hurmph!" Dudley grumbled. "She's not wishing anyone a merry Christmas."

"I beg your pardon," queried Anna.

"Oh, I was just mumbling to myself about not having much Christmas spirit," he responded begrudgingly. Sometimes that woman was beyond explanation to him and this was certainly one of those times. The more he thought about it, the less he liked the idea. Perhaps he should discuss this with Billy Bob before he did anything else. He was the one who paid his fees and he should know what he was paying for.

"Anna, get Billy Bob Whitehall on the phone for me," he said making his decision. He knew Billy Bob's business practices and this was not something he would condone.

After work Savannah changed into a jogging outfit and her running shoes to go see Tom. It gave her a feeling of comfort and reminded her of their days of jogging together, enjoying the great outdoors. It wasn't the same, but permitted her to fanaticize about being with him. And she could comfortably sit and read to him.

She was currently reading *The Fellowship of the Ring* by J.R.R. Tolkien, one of Tom's favorites. He had enjoyed the trilogy in school, but this was his favorite because it dealt with the breaking of the Fellowship when the ring becomes too evil. There was something else that Tom derived from the book because he told Savannah that in life one must be careful to refrain from evil because evil ruins relationships. She often wondered what had jaded Tom about relationships because he was so kind and considerate of her, much like how her mom described her dad. She had never asked for further explanations and wished she had. She had never felt an urgency to know more. Now she saw life differently. She knew there was no guarantee of tomorrow, but just now in the moment. She had learned to cherish each moment of each day. Maybe Tom knew that and that was why he had always preferred the song "Cherished."

"Tom, there is so much more I want to know about you. You have to come back so you can tell me and so we can have the life we dreamed about," she whispered.

Before leaving Tom, Savannah prayed for him out loud and holding his hand, as she did every day. "Lord, I thank You for bringing Tom into my life. I thank You for what he means to me as Your gift of enduring love. I trust You, God, that in all things You will be glorified because You are in control of all creation. Watch over Tom tonight and bring him back to me. Amen."

The rehab center had a quarter mile indoor track for helping patients regain their strength, but often the hospital staff would use the track at off hours for personal training.

During the winter months Savannah was one of the staff who found the track very useful for keeping in shape. It provided a warm, secure place to release stress. Twenty laps was monotonous but it was the best she could do for now. If Tom were with her, they could run outside together. The cold never bothered them because they challenged each other and it was five miles before they were breathing hard.

Life had become complicated for Savannah. She had her routine, but many times a crisis interrupted her routine leaving her scrambling to recover and questioning everything. She had been drawn to public relations because it presented a variety of exciting challenges, some mundane, but most with the volatility of a rollercoaster. Now evil had entered her life without her knowledge and threatened every aspect of her routine. Even the home she and Tom appreciated together was at risk. Ever since Mitch had warned her about meeting with him, she often looked over her shoulder to see what was behind her or watched the shadows more closely for something sinister. Being careful was one thing, but she was beyond vigilant, almost paranoid.

Chapter 20

January 10, winter tore through Jackson leaving behind sheets of ice wreaking havoc for the city dwellers in every way imaginable. Sleet and snow immobilized both Rankin and Hinds Counties and both civil and law authorities cautioned people about dangerous driving conditions. Warnings were posted everywhere for people to stay home. All the schools and many state and local offices closed for the day. Jackson was not equipped to handle a blanket of ice with only a handful of sanding trucks.

But Barbara Whitehall had no intentions of letting a little thing like an ice storm keep her home. At 10 a.m. she had an appointment with Dudley Randall and planned to keep that appointment.

"Barb, did you call to see if Dudley will even be there?" Billy Bob asked as he pulled his overcoat from the closet.

"If he knows what's good for him, he'll be there. He knows how important this is to me and promised he would have it ready today," she replied donning her coat and gloves. It was a special day for her, so she selected a navy blue wool pantsuit with boots for the occasion. Looking good was key for any event, but dressing for this meeting brought her a special delight.

"Yes, but he didn't know how bad the storm was last night. They predicted cold temperatures and the possibility of precipitation. But now there's ice everywhere."

"Look, I want to get the eviction notice, signed, sealed and delivered. He has stalled long enough. I am sure Dudley is on his way to the office, if he isn't there already. Now, let's go."

"Okay, Barb. But I'm telling you, it's not a good idea."

"Billy Bob, will you just get the car and let's be on with it?" she asked emphatically.

Knowing it was a losing battle and if he didn't drive her, she would drive herself, he followed orders. Once on the road he hoped she would see the foolishness of making the trek and they would turn around and come home.

Two blocks from the house the car hit an ice patch on Old Canton Road. With a car as heavy as the Lincoln Continental it was difficult for Billy Bob to keep it from sliding. Fortunately, there was no traffic and he easily corrected the skidding.

"Can't you drive any faster? We need to be there by 10," Barbara fussed as Billy Bob cautiously edged into the curves on Old Canton Road to Northside Drive, which would take them to North State Street and then into the downtown area.

"Look, Barbara, I want to get there in one piece and these streets are just not that safe in these conditions. We just skidded back there."

"Well, that was your fault for taking the curve too fast."

"One minute you tell me to speed up and the next it's that I'm going too fast. So, which is it?"

"I just don't like being out here on these roads."

"We could've stayed home today and waited for the roads to get better."

"No. I want to get this done today. Just watch what you're doing."

"I am, Barb."

Even though there had been absolutely no traffic on the roads, the 30 minute drive was turning into nearly an hour as Billy Bob inched over the ice patches along the treacherous Northside Drive. But bridges normally froze sooner than roadways and the one he was approaching was a solid sheet of ice. Because it was old and used only by the locals, the Eubanks Creek railing was wooden, not the metal normally found on city bridges. Billy Bob was taking his time as he approached the bridge. He could see it reflecting the light, but wasn't sure if it was just wet or ice.

As the car approached the bridge, he confirmed it wasn't water reflecting the light, but ice covering the wooden planks. Without traction the right front tire skidded causing the vehicle to veer to the right. Speed wasn't a factor, just the physics of more than 5,000 pounds of force against an old wooden guardrail. The railing never stood a chance with the car sliding sideways, splintering pieces of old oak into an assembly of contorted spears. The two front tires hung over the frozen creek.

"Billy Bob, I told you to be careful. Now look what you've done!" screamed Barbara as she fidgeted in her seat.

"Be still, Barb. You'll send us over the edge."

"Don't yell at me," she retorted leaning forward.

"Don't move, Barb."

It was too late, she was leaning down to get her phone out of her purse. The shift of the weight in the car with the motor still running tipped it towards the ice below.

Billy Bob put the car in reverse, but the change in the transmission caused it to teeter more. The car began sliding toward the ice with more wooden boards creaking and splitting. He tried to put it in park.

"Billy Bob, do something!"

"Unfasten your seat belt," he instructed as he began to unbuckle his own. If he couldn't get the car to go in reverse, at least they could get out.

"I can't. You have to help me."

Keeping his left hand on the steering wheel, Billy Bob reached over to unfasten Barb's seatbelt with his right hand. His movement shifted the car even more towards the creek. Then slowly the vehicle plummeted, hood first, into slabs of frozen ice. With the winter rains causing it to rise above flood-levels, the creek that was normally only six or seven feet deep now measured at nearly 12 feet. The car quickly pierced the sheet of ice like a missile being launched in the wrong direction. Taking in water the engine sputtered and died. Billy Bob pulled on the door handle, but it wouldn't budge. He reached over to Barb's door, but it was locked and he couldn't get the handle to move. Mud trapped his door since the car landed partially on the driver's side. There was no way to get his door open. They had to get out on Barbara's side.

With the seatbelt still securely fastened, Barbara began thrashing wildly. In her fidgeting and twisting to unlatch her seat belt, Barbara slammed her head against the door, fracturing the glass. Small cracks allowed the creek to seep into the car even faster. Billy Bob's dearth under the tilted steering wheel pinned him to his seat as the force of the water rushed in through crevices that widened in the window. Then he saw Barb loose her struggle with the seatbelt and her body went limp.

He knew he only had seconds to get them out, but with her head injury Barbara was dead weight and he could not budge her. His futile efforts to move her or reach over her to get the door open only exacerbated the situation. He managed to angle the steering wheel up, but couldn't maneuver his body into the back seat. He wanted to open the passenger door, but the child safety lock was on. Running out of air, running out of ideas and running out of time, he was stuck. She was out cold. Seconds ticked away like hours and yet he made no progress.

Trapped in the vehicle, stuck in the freezing sludge with ice cold water rushing through the fractured window, they faced the onset of hypothermia. Billy Bob became disoriented as the numbness engulfed his body. It was almost euphoric and calming compared to the thrashing and flailing of arms and legs only seconds before. He was thankful that Barb had not suffered more. Hitting her head and knocking her out lessened the anguish of her ordeal. Billy Bob looked at his beloved, bent over and leaning against the door. She looked peaceful. Billy Bob closed his eyes for the last time.

Then there was no more. No more sound of heavy breathing. No more movement indicating life. No more efforts to exit. There was stillness, cold, frozen stiffness. The silver luxury sedan sat in silence and solitude cocooning the couple in a coffin of coldness.

At 10:30 Dudley called the Whitehall house and spoke to Pearl.

"Mr. Randall, they should be there by now," she explained. "They left here before 9 o'clock. As far as I know, they were not going anywhere else."

"Okay, Pearl. Thanks. Would you have one of them call me as soon as you hear from them?"

Dudley placed the phone in its cradle. He shook his head. This was not like Barbara Whitehall to be late, especially to pick up something as important as a copy of the eviction notice. He had made it to his office without incident in his four-wheel drive Honda CRV. The roads had been treacherous and he had told Anna not to come in. But he knew Barbara would be there, come hail or high water. But this was an ice storm and he was concerned for the Whitehalls. He had been successful in convincing Billy Bob to hold off on the eviction notice until after Christmas, but he was sure that it had not been an easy task for him. So where was she? He had already sent the notice to the Rankin County Constable's office. He anticipated the constable would serve the papers tomorrow evening.

Hours passed while the silver Lincoln rested on the driver's side in the creek bed. A deputy from Hinds County drove slowly down North State Street and stopped when he saw the damaged guardrail. Even with his Smokey Bear hat protecting his head and the lined raincoat over his jacket, he was still freezing as he stepped out of the patrol car. Examining the broken rails and the edge of the bridge he spotted a hole in the thick sheet of ice that stretched across the creek.

"This does not look good," he mumbled and shook his head. Back in his warm car, he called the dispatcher and reported the accident requesting divers, a tow truck and notification to the coroner's office. Some of the roads were becoming more passable with sanding trucks out in force. Still this was a lesser traveled road and getting emergency equipment here took time.

The recovery operation took several hours before the car was extracted from the frozen muck. Only then did the county Mounty provide the license plate to the dispatcher for her to make identification. Immediately phone calls were made to JPD and Chief Bennett, who personally knew the next-of-kin and took responsibility for making that notification. The Whitehalls would make the news as soon as their identity was transmitted over the police scanner. The chief knew he needed to make his call quickly.

"Savannah, this is Chief Bennett," said the solemn voice through the telephone wires. "Tom's parents have been in an accident."

"Oh, no. Are they okay?"

"No, I'm sorry to tell you this—perhaps I should have come in person, but I wanted to let you know as soon as possible, they were both killed when their car went off the bridge over Eubanks Creek. We're sure it's them, but I need you to make the positive identification at the University's morgue. Are you at the hospital now?

"No, I didn't go in with the streets so icy. Non-essential people were told not to report to the hospital today."

"I thought so. Can you come meet me there or would you rather I send a car for you?"

"No, I can drive myself. It will take some time and I'll need to call Tom's brother in Biloxi. This is just awful."

"Why don't you make the positive identification before you call his brother? We're sure it is them, but we must have a family member corroborate it. Okay?"

"Okay. I didn't think of that. I'll be there as soon as I can. I'll see you there."

"Yes, bye."

Before leaving home, Savannah did make a quick call to Pearl and asked her not to pass on the information until she had confirmed the report. But Pearl knew it was them or else they would have been at Mr. Randall's office. She broke her promise not to call anyone by letting their lawyer know. There were many things Pearl knew because she often overheard conversations in the Whitehall household—things like why they were on the way to see the lawyer, things that Savannah wouldn't know, and things that would change both women's lives. Pearl had to do the right thing and that meant letting Mr. Randall know now.

At the morgue Savannah made the identification just like she had for Wanda last year. She had seen many family members making those crucial pronouncements in the ER of the medical center and then lapse into despair. It was difficult to see someone you cared about lying on a slab and knowing they would never speak again, never smile again or breathe again. Her heart ached for Tom, but she was glad she was the one at the morgue and not him or his brother.

"I need to call Willie," she said to the chief, who had been watching her expression or lack thereof.

"I'll go with you," he replied leading her back upstairs of the hospital. "I take it you have done this kind of thing before?"

"Yes, but why do you say that?"

"Just an observation. Most people's reaction is more of a shock at seeing a dead body."

"Well, I do work here and although we try to save lives, there are plenty that don't make it. Unfortunately, I get to see them, too."

"I see," he said opening the door to the reception area of her office. "I'll be out here if you need me."

"Thank you," she said as she opened her private office door.

The phone call to Willie was not easy. She reached him at his office, where he usually was. A chip off the old block as a workaholic, he was highly compensated for his efforts. One of his goals was to make more money than his dad, unlike Tom who was not interested in the money, but wanted to make a difference in the world. The two boys were alike in many ways, but with a distinct difference in motivation.

"I know this is all a shock, Willie, but we will need to think about the funeral service and obituaries and notifying your dad's lawyer."

"Yeah, it's a bit much to deal with right now. I'll get Becky and the kids together and drive up to Jackson in the morning. We'll stay at their house. Maybe you can meet us there tomorrow afternoon?"

"Sure. Do you have any idea what funeral home to contact?"

"I'm sure it's Baldwin's, but do you want me to take care of that?"

"It's just that I think it would be better to move them from the morgue and if I can contact the right place, that will just be another step completed. None of this will be easy and I will do as much as I can."

"Thanks, Savannah. Yeah, go ahead and contact Baldwin's. I'll see you tomorrow, then."

The accident made the front page of the *Clarion-Ledger* the next morning although arrangements and details were sketchy. In Mississippi the Whitehalls were a power couple with Billy Bob's money and Barbara's charity and social activities. The article speculated as to what would happen to the dealership empire he had amassed, but little was mentioned about Tom. Willie, with his automotive fortune in Biloxi, was mentioned as the heir apparent.

Willie, Savannah and Dudley made the arrangements for the Whitehalls' services at First Baptist Church and the burial at Woodlawn Cemetery exactly one week after the fatal accident. The sanctuary held 2,000 and was nearly standing room only. Both U.S. senators and one of the U.S. representatives spoke briefly at the service led by Dr. Barton. The funeral procession stopped traffic for an hour as it meandered from the church on North State Street to the cemetery on Robinson Road. Not many non-political figures attracted as much of a gathering as did Barbara and Billy Bob, who were buried side by side at the same time, the way they had lived their lives.

The lawyer took Savannah aside after the burial and said she needed to come by his office. He had unfinished business with the Whitehalls that needed her attention.

Chapter 21

With the funeral behind her, Savannah concentrated on Tom. Dr. Roddenburg and Dr. Pendleton had both given her excellent reports about Tom. Pendleton was extremely encouraged by her visits to Tom and his responses. If they could unlock his mind and wake him up, he just knew Tom could make a full recovery. Savannah credited her daily prayers with making a difference. God was at work and somehow He would be glorified through this.

Savannah was back to her regular routine of visiting Tom. She was reading from Psalms 100 to 121 when she stopped to stroke Tom's forehead.

"*I will lift up my eyes unto the hills from whence cometh my help. My help cometh from the Lord,*" she quoted. "*My help cometh from the Lord,*" she repeated gently rubbing his eyebrows.

His eyes fluttered as they had many times when she spoke lovingly to him, but then they opened. She could see the sparkle of life in them as he looked straight at her for the first time in months.

"Hey, Babe," were the almost inaudible words from his lips. She wasn't sure she really heard them. But he spoke again, "I'm thirsty."

Yes, she did hear him, she saw his lips move.

"Tom, you're awake. Oh my God! You're really awake!"

"Yeah, I'm awake, but where am I? And why are you so surprised?"

"You are in the hospital and have been in a coma for more than 10 months."

"A coma? What do you mean?"

Savannah explained what happened months ago, and then abruptly stopped. "I have to tell the doctors. They will be so excited."

She called the nurse and asked for Doctors Pendleton and Roddenburg to come.

"Tell me more. What are all these contraptions above my bed?"

"Tom there is so much to tell you, but right now we have to celebrate with the two doctors who have been keeping you alive."

Both doctors raced into the room. They were more excited than Savannah and wanted to prod and poke Tom.

"Whoa, doc!" exclaimed Tom. "I'm awake and need to catch up. It seems I've missed quite a lot in the last 10 months."

"We know," agreed Roddenburg, "but I want to see if my therapy worked and you can move your arms and legs."

The doctors worked with Tom and were amazed at how well he responded to their tests, both physical and mental. Both were recording every movement, every response and every achievement of Tom. Their plans were a joint success story for the American Journal of Science and Medicine and any other accolades that might come with it. They were talking so fast, Tom had to slow them down.

"Hey, doc, I appreciate all you have done for me, but I'm not a guinea pig nor am I sure about all this attention," Tom pleaded.

"Don't you realize that you're medical history in the making? We don't always get success stories like this to share with the world. Just ask Savannah. She's been after us to show the world our new facility here. Now we have you as the realization of determination," explained Pendleton.

The two doctors raved on goaded by their egos and success with Tom. Savannah was relegated to the sidelines as the doctors had Tom sit, stand and take his first step. They were amazed by his abilities, even though they had both predicted this could happen. Hours later they realized Tom was exhausted and needed to rest and left scribbling on their charts.

"Are you hungry?" Savannah asked.

"I'm too tired to eat right now, but could you bring me a big juicy hamburger from McDonald's tomorrow?"

"I'm sure that can be arranged. Anything else?"

"Yes. Some fries, a coke and a strawberry shake."

"That's a lot for someone who hasn't had a meal in months. But I will bring it. I am just so happy to have you back."

"Me, too," he barely mouthed before falling asleep.

Savannah slipped out of the room nearly frolicking down the hallways and out to her car, praising God all the way. The first thing she did when she got home was to call her mom with the good news. So many prayers had been answered in one day, she was too excited to sleep, but when it did come, it was the most restful sleep she had experienced in a very long time.

Checking on Tom before going to her office, she realized he would have a busy day with Pendleton and Roddenburg. She was surprised they weren't in the hospital room before her.

"Good morning, hon," she said to her barely awake husband.

"Hey, babe. Where's my hamburger?"

"Is that all you can think about—food?"

"No, how about a kiss?"

"Now that's better," she responded with a quick kiss on the lips. "Let me fluff your pillow for you."

"I could get used to this treatment," he said reaching up to put his arms around her.

"Just make sure I'm the only one you get this special treatment from."

"Oh, I will, for sure."

She spent a few minutes with Tom before the nurse came in and shooed her out because she places to take him today.

Back in her office there was one important phone call for her to make before plowing into her day. She called Chief Bennett, who was extremely interested in how lucid Tom appeared and what he remembered.

"When can I talk to Tom?" he asked.

"Why don't you come by around lunch time and bring him a hamburger, French fries, a Coke and a strawberry shake," she replied.

"That's all?" he asked and chuckled.

"Well, it was an order he placed last night, and I'm not sure how much he can actually eat, but I'm sure he'd like to try."

Not to show up empty handed, the chief complied with Tom's request.

"Hey, officer, good to see you back among the alive and kicking," the chief greeted the young man he thought was gone.

"Good to be among the living, sir. And I see you must have been talking to my wife," he said eyeing the contraband.

"Yep, she called this morning and I would have been here sooner, but she said you would be out getting tested."

"If you call it that. It's more like being stuck a hundred times and prodded where prods shouldn't go. I can't wait to get out of here."

"Well, take it easy. You've a lot of catching up to do. You can start with quenching your junk food appetite and then we can get down to business. I need to know what you remember about your accident."

"Unfortunately, I don't remember much about that day. It's still hazy for me. Savannah filled in the details she remembers from her arrival at the training site, but none of it makes sense to me. I can't imagine why that bar gave way with me. I know from what she said that someone sawed it almost in two, but that's all I can tell you, sir. I wish I knew more."

"We've been able to piece together how it was cut and even have a good line on who, but not the why. What can you tell me about Chris O'Donnell?"

"We go back a long way to high school. We were acquaintances, never what you'd call friends even though our paths frequently crossed. There was something that I just didn't trust about him. It was never anything I could put my finger on until we did a drug bust at a nightclub a few years ago. We had just swarmed the doors and Chris showed up behind me. He wasn't in his SWAT gear, but in street clothes. He claimed to have heard the action going down on the radio and came to 'help out'. First of all, we had maintained radio silence and placed the two teams at both entrances. His presence was just suspicious, but I couldn't prove anything."

"Did you report your suspicions?"

"Just to my supervisor, because that was all they were. And I didn't want to unjustly accuse a fellow officer. But I did keep my eyes on him. I started keeping a journal with info on when I would see him 'show up' at drug busts, which happened more and more often. I didn't say anything, because he is a cop and when he went to IA, it limited who I could report him to. So I just kept my journal. One day I was writing in it and he saw me and asked what I was doing. I tried to shrug him off, but he became persistent. I started noticing that he would write in a notebook when he saw me. And I thought, 'oh great, now IA will investigate me.' But nothing ever happened. And I never seemed to be able to get anything solid on him, just a lot of coincidental incidents. About a week before the accident, my journal went missing."

"Did you ever find it?"

"Yes, the day before our competition it showed up in my locker."

"Was anything missing out of it?"

"No, because I never used names or locations, just codes that only I would recognize. So, I thought everything was cool and I would eventually get enough on him or prove him innocent."

"Did Savannah tell you that he had been arrested?"

"No, she didn't. When? For what?"

"We finally got him for a drug deal at Cat Ballew. A PI hired by your parents was able to get enough evidence for the arrest at the end of October. Now if we could get you to translate your notes, we can add significant dates to his drug dealings. And you can testify at his trial with this additional info."

Tom and the chief continued to discuss the case they were making against Chris for his attempted murder charge. They were soon interrupted by doctors and interns gawking at the latest miracle at the teaching facility. The chief aptly took his exit cue.

As regular as clockwork, Savannah came to visit Tom, but this time she didn't do all the talking. Their conversation was two-way, the best way for communication to take place. It changed her visits drastically. She still read to him, but now there was a real conversation.

"Tomorrow Mr. Randall, your parents' attorney, needs to talk to you. Are you up for it?"

"I don't see why not. Is this about my dad's will and the estate?"

"Well, that is part of it, but there is more."

Savannah filled in the details for Tom about the divorce proceedings, the planned eviction notice and how Barbara moved him to Atlanta and back to Jackson to obtain guardianship for his medical and physical well-being. Fortunately, the lawyer had stayed the eviction notice when the Whitehalls were killed, but Tom needed to nullify the divorce and the guardianship. Both could be accomplished with a notarized signature, but required immediate attention.

Tom was incensed by what his mother had instigated. "How did she ever get dad to go along with this?" he raged.

"I really don't think your dad was a part of it. He was the one who invited me to Atlanta to bring you back. He tried to thwart some of her actions, but acquiesced to the rest. It is just hard to swallow that she hated me that much."

"Hey, Babe, it wasn't you. She has always had a mean streak. Growing up I could see it when she did things behind my dad's back. I think it was the money that turned her into an ogre. You know like what happened to Frodo when the Fellowship was broken because of the ring. The money was evil in her hands and severed relationships for her."

"Yes, I just read that book to you. Do you remember? It was while you were still in the coma."

"Really? No wonder it seems so fresh to me. Did you read to me a lot?"

"Yes, every day I was with you. Dr. Pendleton thinks this was part of the healing for you. And getting you back from Atlanta helped with this."

"How in the world did you manage to keep your sanity with all this going on?"

"I trusted God to see me through it all and He did. I prayed a lot and knew that somehow justice would win. It always does in the hands of our mighty God. There is a Scripture that epitomizes this.

"The prophet Amos is chastising Israel for making a show of serving God while committing unholy acts and prophesizes that the Day of the Lord will come and judgment will come because God does not want superficial sacrifices, but true worship. After all the warnings and woes Amos says to the Israelites, '*But let justice roll like a river, righteousness like a never failing stream.*' You see, right and justice will prevail under God's plan. I don't think your mom and dad dying was justice, but I do believe justice has been served by preventing what she intended to harm us. It wasn't that she wanted to harm you, but in her efforts to separate us, it would have harmed you. Bringing you back to Jackson was the best thing she could do. She just didn't know it. We judge from our perspective, but God judges from His omniscience."

But let justice roll like a river, righteousness like a never-failing stream.—Amos 5:24